The Seeker

His Dreamseekers

Book 2

By

Ronna M. Bacon

And you will seek Me and find Me, when you search
for Me with all your heart.
Jeremiah 29:13. NKJV

I sought the Lord, and He heard me, And delivered
me from all my fears.
Psalms 34:4. NKJV

Table of Contents

Chapter 1

His eyes blinking open and closed, Taggart Rafferty shifted on the hospital bed that he was lying on, not quite awake and definitely not sure where he was. A hand was raised to rub at his face, the days' old stubble rough under his shaky hand. He sighed to himself, losing that small grip he had on reality as he drifted off again, this time to a real sleep and not a drugged sleep. He had been there a week, kept sedated as he kept trying to rise and leave. Tag, as he was affectionately known as, needed that sleep. His fellow officers had found him, beaten and unconscious in a little travelled area of a local park. Tag had been on duty the day before he was found and hadn't reported in as required. A search had taken over a day to find him. His patrol vehicle had been found in a small village nowhere near where he was, his utility belt and radio dumped inside the locked vehicle. There had been no signs of a struggle, which puzzled the responding officers.

The physician treating him just shook his head at the nurse before he reached to bring up Tag's chart on the computer he was working on.

"He's been awake?"

"Just barely. He kept muttering a name but none of us can catch it, his voice is too low. He keeps trying to get up and find someone. At least, that's what it seems like." Betty, the nurse on duty, studied

—
6

the man on the hospital bed. "Who would do this, James?"

James O'Connor, the physician, just shook his head. "I have no idea, Betty. Until Tag awakens, none of us will know."

A day later, Tag was awake and on his feet, shaking his head at Betty.

"I'm leaving, Betty." He refused to stay, as shaky on his feet as he was. Something or someone, he thought, was driving him to leave the hospital. He needed to find someone, a lady, he thought, who was in trouble. Tag just couldn't remember where she was and that made him afraid. Little in life did that, serving as a police officer for a number of years had taken that fear from him. Until now. And just who was he seeking for?

Tag turned at last, dressed and ready to leave. He knew that he should stay but just couldn't. Not when someone needed his help. He stared at his friend, Stephen Gordon, who stood, waiting for him to decide if he wanted the wheelchair or not. Tag moved at last towards the door, not seeing James standing outside in the hall, shaking his head.

"He's leaving, Betty?"

"He is, James. He is refusing to stay. He says he has to find someone. Only he can't tell us who."

"A lady, likely, Betty, given the way that he's acting. Did he get all his paperwork?" James had had a good idea that Tag would do just what he did and had prepared for that eventuality.

Stephen followed Tag into his house, his eyes searching for anything that was off and not seeing anything. He shook his head as Tag headed for his bedroom and clean clothes. Stephen himself headed for the kitchen, reaching for the coffee pot to make the coffee that he knew Tag would want and then the toaster, finding a loaf of bread in the fridge.

Tag stood for a moment, his eyes on the closed bathroom door, before he sighed. *This wasn't such a good idea, was it, Lord? I'm still weak and shaky but I need to find her. She's in danger and I just don't know where to start looking. Stephen would help me and I need him to.*

Staring at his left hand, Tag shook his head. He had avoided having his fellow officers seeing the band on his left ring finger. He could vaguely remember it being put there, a threat to the lady leaving little doubt in his mind that if he didn't marry her, then she would be killed. Just why that was, he didn't or couldn't remember.

Showered, shaved and in clean clothes, Tag hesitated again as he walked down the hallway towards the kitchen, his head bowing as he prayed once more for the lady that he had to find. Only he had no idea how to do just that.

Stephen watched his friend closely as Tag reached to pour his coffee and then stood, his head down, his hands flat on the granite countertop. He stared at Tag's left hand, his mouth opening to ask a question before he snapped it closed. *Just what had happened to my friend, Lord? And how do I help him?*

—

"Tag?" Stephen's voice, though quiet, held the questions that he needed to ask and wouldn't.

"Stephen? Can we eat and then pray? I need help and I am not sure just how to ask for it."

"Sure. I have toast ready for you." Stephen watched closely as Tag sank gratefully down into his chair, his mug of coffee hitting the table.

Tag stared at the toast, his stomach roiling within him as fleeting images flickered in his memory. He ran a hand through his light brown hair and then closed the dark brown eyes that held too many of his thoughts at the present moment.

Stephen raised his head at long last, having spent time in prayer with Tag, not quite sure why Tag had prayed as he had.

"Tag? What happened? You were found miles away from your vehicle. Your utility belt and radio were found in it. Your uniform shirt as well."

Tag nodded before he sipped at his coffee.

"That's what I thought, Stephen. I can't remember everything, but there is a lady out there that I need to find. She's in danger and I don't know why." He stared at his clasped hands before he raised the left one. "I had to do this, Stephen. I just had to. They threatened to kill her if I didn't. That's why I was beaten. I had refused until I just had to agree. God help me, I had to. Now I have to find her."

Stephen stared at him, dumbfounded, not sure how to respond. His mouth opened and closed a few times before he found his voice.

—

"Tag? Who is she? And just where is she?" Stephen waited, knowing Tag well enough to know his friend would respond.

"I don't know, Stephen. I just don't know." Tag reached for his wallet, opening it to pull out a folded paper. A picture fell from it. "This is she. And this is the marriage license. It's registered, I know that. They showed me that before they dumped me in that park."

Stephen reached for the paper and the photo, studying both.

"What actually happened, Tag? How did they get you to go with them? It's against our training to do that."

"I know, Stephen. I had pulled in there for a break, to eat my lunch. I saw her running towards me and stepped out of the vehicle to speak with her. As I was, the men approached, two vehicles blocking me in. Before I could reach for my radio, they had me on the ground. I was forced to remove my belt and radio and lock them in the car. I prayed that the radio would work and dispatch could find the vehicle."

"We didn't get it on the radio, but John found your car shortly after you had left it, we think." Stephen stared at the window for a moment. "Then what?"

"We were forced into one of the vehicles and driven around for a while. They took us to the old Baker homestead near the highway. The lady was scared, Stephen, petrified is how I would describe it. We weren't together for much of the first couple of hours. The men returned, forced us into one room and made their demands. I can remember her refusing and me refusing. That's when the beatings started." Tag's face contorted briefly as he remembered the blows that he had taken and his hand felt for his ribs. "I don't know why they threatened to kill her. They never said. She tried to escape, I do know that. A minister appeared at that point, I think, and was forced to marry us. He tried to refuse but his family was threatened. The deed was done, as they say. I don't remember much after that."

Stephen sat in silence, his eyes on the photo.

"What's her name?"

"Her name? Ayron Avery, pronounced E-rin. She's beautiful, Stephen. I need to find her. I need to take care of her. And I need to determine what and who is after her." His head turned as he heard a sound at the back door and was on his feet, moving that way, ignoring the twinges of pain he felt, Stephen at his heels.

Cautiously opening the door, Tag stood and stared at the lady standing there before he reached to draw her inside and to a chair, sinking back into his own. His eyes took in the raven curls that reached down the lady's back and the violet eyes that held pain and hope and questions.

"Ayron? How? You're here?" Tag was puzzled how she had managed to do just that. He didn't think that they had exchanged addresses. At least, he didn't think that they had.

Ayron Avery stared at the man who she didn't know but who was her husband, seeing the bruising that had turned to a garish colour and then begun to fade. She saw the worry for her in his eyes that he was trying hard to hide, but she also saw the character of the man in how he sat and how he held himself and how he watched her ever so closely. *How did that happen, Lord? Is this the plan that You have for me? A plan to keep me safe as I seek to find the men responsible for whatever it seems that I am now involved in?*

"Taggart? You're alive. They told me that you were dead. I didn't believe them. I don't know how I got away, but I think that they let me. I heard them talking about you being in the hospital and tried to get in to see you but there was always someone around. I heard your friend talking about taking you home and found a taxi so that I could follow you." Tears welled in her eyes. "Please, Tag? Can you help me?" With that, her eyes closed and she slid from her chair, Tag's arms reaching for her before he was on his feet, heading for the living room and gently laying her on the couch. He reached for a blanket to tuck around her, taking with thanks the pillow that Stephen handed him and raising her head enough to slip it underneath, his hand brushing down her hair, a prayer raising for her.

Stephen stood and watched, a frown on his face, before he was outside, searching for anything that would help solve the mystery. His head shook as he remembered her words. What had Tag gotten involved in anyway?

Tag stood and watched Ayron, his heart already taken without him being aware of that fact. All he knew was that he had to help this lady, who appeared to be his bride, and he had no idea how to do that.

Chapter 2

Late that afternoon, Tag roused from where he had been dozing in his easy chair. He knew that he should have stretched out on his bed, to get the rest that James had ordered him to get, but he just couldn't. He just couldn't leave Ayron. His eyes studied her before he was on his feet, heading for the kitchen, squinting at the clock, his headache making it difficult to see. A hand on the coffee pot as he started a fresh pot, Tag turned, not sure what Ayron liked to drink. He sighed. *Lord, this is not going anywhere. Not yet. I don't know anything about this lady, my bride, but You do. Please lead me in how I approach this. I am out in the depths of the sea, I feel like, with this. I need to seek Your protection for her, Your guidance in how we proceed, and Your wisdom in finding the ones responsible.*

His phone caught his attention from where he had left it on the table and he reached for it, pausing as he thought through the events earlier that day. Tag knew that Stephen had reached out to his cousin, with his thanks, to shop for clothing and whatever else Ayron needed at the present time. She had had no luggage and he stopped, realizing that he had no idea what town she was even from. Tag frowned at that thought, a troubled look on his face as he prayed once more for his bride. The bags of clothing that Stephen had returned with were even now in the spare room, waiting for Ayron. Sighing, Tag wondered if he had made a mistake, agreeing that Sarah could shop for Ayron.

Scrolling through his messages, Tag gave a quick grin at the one from Flannery, his friend, Evan's wife. She was worried about him, she said, and just what had he been up to and where had he been? And why hadn't he asked them for help? He sent off a quick text to both Flannery and Evan, knowing that Evan would contact him over the next twenty-four hours. Tag paused and then nodded. Just maybe Evan could help. He knew that Flannery would, but they lived miles away from him. They had gone through an adventure, he thought, and Evan just might have some advice for him. He would certainly pray for Tag. A thought crossed his mind that just maybe he should move up there. He liked the area and could likely find work. Tag just wasn't sure that he could continue in police work. For now, he had to be off on sick leave and that time would be spent in prayer, he knew, regarding what his future plans would be. It seemed that he now had someone else to consider in those very plans.

Heading back to the other room, Tag stood for a moment, his eyes troubled as he watched Ayron. His supervisor, Eric, had been in touch and planned to drop in that evening. Tag had hesitated to tell Eric what he had been through. Who the men were? That he had no idea. He didn't remember seeing them. Tag sighed to himself. This kept getting bigger and bigger and more weird. *Lord, how do I do this? How do I protect Ayron and myself and find out what is going on? I never expected to marry, certainly not this way. You know, Lord, exactly where we're heading, don't You? This You had planned before time started,*

14

didn't You, Lord? Help us, Lord. Help me, Lord, to protect this lady.

Dropping down to the floor beside the couch, Tag watched as Ayron slept, studying the whiteness of her face, the dark circles under her eyes. He was worried, to put it mildly, that it had been hours since she collapsed and had not roused. If she didn't soon, then he would need to awaken her. His arm around her, he reached with gentle fingers to brush back her hair from her face and tuck it behind her ear. He felt the curls, amazed at the softness of her hair between his fingers. His eyes traced the faint bruising on her cheek before he gently touched the fading yellow and green. Tag rested his arm on his upraised knee, a troubled look on his face. A sigh was driven from him even as he reached for her left hand, his thumb rubbing against the wedding band before a thought drove him to his feet and to find his phone.

"Jeff? It's Tag. Yeah, I'm home. Still recuperating. Listen. I know that it's late. You're still at your store? You are? Good. Why? I know I don't buy jewelry. Or at least I didn't." Tag bit at his lip, suddenly unsure of himself, totally out of character for him. "I need some jewelry, Jeff." Tag gave a brief laugh. "Yeah, I do. A wedding band for a lady and a matching one for me. Yes, I did say a wedding band. It's a long story, and I'm sure I'll need your help. Gold?" Tag moved to where he could watch Ayron, seeing her stirring as she awoke. "Rose gold, engraved. And an engagement ring. Ruby, you say? No, I don't think so. What stone do you have in a dark blue or violet? Her eyes are violet and I would like to match that." Tag sighed, knowing that he had to talk to Ayron about changing their bands.

—

Something was driving him to do just that. "You will? I'll be home. Thanks, Jeff."

Setting his phone on the table, Tag moved back towards Ayron, glancing at the clock. He would soon need to decide on what they could or would eat. He really didn't know what he had any more in the freezer or even what his bride liked to eat.

Sitting up abruptly, Ayron searched the room for her captors, fear on her face. Her heart thudded with it as she heard footsteps and refused to look up. She wondered as the man sat beside her on the couch, his hand held out for her to take. Ayron finally reached for it, sensing that she didn't need to fear the man. She heard his whispered prayer for just her, for peace, for protection, for wisdom, for healing, and wondered that her captors would be praying. The only way that they used God's name was as a curse word.

At long last, her eyes raised to study the man beside her, finding his eyes closed as he just sat, her hand held tightly in his. She drew a deep sigh of relief. It was Tag, she thought. She was safe. Or was she? That she really wasn't sure of, not any more. And Ayron really had no idea of why she had been taken captive and held or why she had been forced to marry Tag. That was something she knew that she would be delving into.

Tag's head turned towards her and a smile lit up his face.

"You're awake, Ayron. I thought that you would sleep until tomorrow."

"What time is it?"

"Just after four. You've been sleeping, something I suspect that you really needed." Tag's head tilted so that he could watch her face. "Did it help?"

"It did." Ayron sighed. "But a shower and clean clothes would help. I gather you have a shower, but I have no clean clothes."

"That I can help with. Stephen had his cousin do some shopping for you, just until we can get out and do that." He stood, pulling her to her feet, and then leading her to the spare bedroom that he had designated as hers. "Here. Take a look at what she got. We weren't sure on colours or styles, but I pray that she did all right. Sarah told me that she threw in a bunch of stuff, personal care, I think is how she worded it. She's willing to help you, if you need it."

Ayron stared at the bags on the bed before looking up at her oh-so-tall groom. *How do I do this, Lord? How do I continue to live here, putting him at risk?*

"Thank you, Tag. This should work." She pulled her hand free to walk over and open the bags, drawing out the clothes, a soft sound coming from her.

Tag's heart dropped. *We blew it, didn't we, Lord? I should have waited.* Surprised to find Ayron back in his space, his hands reached for her shoulders. Ayron was not content with that, reaching instead to hug him and then moving back to choose what she wanted to wear.

—

17

"Take all the time you need, love. I'll look at finding something for supper for us." Tag bit at his lip. "I don't know what you like to eat or drink."

"Tea is good, if you have it. Juice? As to food, I'm not really that picky, but I just can't abide cauliflower or broccoli or cooked cabbage."

A glint of mischief gleamed in Tag's eyes as he hid his smile.

"Here, that's exactly what I was going to cook." He watched as she spun to face him, a narrowed look to her eyes before she shook a finger at him. "Seriously? Stephen did some grocery shopping for us. I can grill some chicken and do a tossed salad?"

"That works. Thanks, Tag. And just who is Stephen?"

"Stephen is a fellow officer and a good friend." Tag heard the doorbell ring. "And I need to talk to you about our rings. I asked a friend who has a jewelry store to bring us new ones. I just don't like the feeling that I am getting about these ones." He stared at his hand, missing the look on her face.

"You don't?" When Tag shook his head, Ayron drew a deep breath. "Can we get rid of these ones? I think I remember one of the men talking about being able to track us. Is that how?"

Tag's eyes shot to hers. "They said that? Then, we'll get rid of them."

Chapter 3

Shutting the front door behind him, Sergeant Eric Bishop stood for a moment, his head tilted as he listened. He frowned to himself as he walked towards the kitchen where he could hear Tag moving around. He watched Tag closely, seeing the emotions that Tag was trying hard to hide.

"Eric? Here. Have a seat." Tag set the mug of tea on the table in front of the chair that Eric had chosen and then sat himself, a mug of coffee grasped tightly in his hands. He had no idea of how to proceed, to talk to Eric, a man who he had little difficulty talking to in a normal setting. But then again, this was far from a normal setting.

"Tag? How are you?" Eric assessed him, seeing the way Tag shifted in his chair. This was not Tag. He was one of the most calm and collected of his officers, able to engage people and walk into situations and settle everything and everyone down.

"I really don't know, Eric. I really don't know." Tag looked up, an expression on his face that was unreadable. "I've gotten into a situation that I have no idea where it's heading."

Nodding, Eric sipped at his tea. "Talk to me, Tag. You never had a problem doing that."

"I know, Eric. This time? It involves someone else." Tag studied his hands, his eyes on the ring that Ayron had placed there not that long before.

—

Ayron had been surprised when she saw the rings that Jeff had left. She had remained out of sight while Tag was speaking with Jeff, knowing that he needed to meet his friend this way. Tag had gone looking for her a short while after Jeff left, studying her closely. She is on the edge of breaking, Tag thought. He had reached for her hand, to exchange the wedding band and add the engagement ring. He had approved of the ones that Jeff had brought to him, choosing a blue star sapphire from the selection provided. Tag had kissed the back of her hand when he was finished before stepping back, his eyes on her. That they needed to talk, both knew this, but right now was not the time. Not when Tag was expecting his supervisor to appear.

Eric shifted on his chair to look towards the hallway as he heard soft footsteps and then saw Tag rise and head that way. He couldn't understand the low voices but stood as Tag appeared with Ayron, her hand tight in his. A puzzled look crossed Eric's face.

When Tag didn't speak, Eric opened and closed his mouth. He studied the couple and then saw their hands and the wedding bands. When did this happen, he wondered? Tag wasn't dating anyone. That Eric knew as Tag had been adamant his was too dangerous an occupation to be married. He had shrugged off the fact that he knew officers who were married and simply grinned at Eric when he commented on that.

"Tag? Who is this? Care to introduce me to the lady?" Eric moved back to his chair as Tag seated Ayron, setting her cup of tea in front of her.

"Eric? This is Ayron Avery Rafferty." He looked up as Eric made a muted sound. "We were

———

20

married the day that I disappeared. It's a short story in some ways, but we have no idea who or why. The beating I took? That was to make me agree to marry Ayron. If I had refused, they would have killed her. I couldn't let that happen."

Eric stared at Tag and then at Ayron, finding Ayron looking at her mug of tea.

"The beating? And then they dumped you? That doesn't make sense, Tag."

"I know that it doesn't. We had never met before this. I don't know why they targeted us. All I know is that day, I saw Ayron running towards me, got out to speak with her, and then was forced to leave my equipment in the car." He frowned. "I don't get why the shirt."

"So no one could identify you as an officer, I suspect. Did you state all this in your statement?" Eric studied the younger couple closely.

"I did, Eric." Tag reached for Ayron's hand. "She's the one I was trying to get up and find. They must have dropped her near the hospital. Ayron says that she heard Stephen talking with someone and then followed me here. She has nothing with her, Eric."

"Sarah did some shopping for you?" Eric smiled at Tag's nod. "She likes to do that. Ayron, may I call you that?" He waited until Ayron raised her head, looked at him, and then nodded. "Okay. So over the next couple of days, I will have one of our detectives come by. Tag's not back at work until he is cleared. They'll talk to you and start an investigation."

21

"Thank you." Ayron's voice was low but the two men could see how troubled she was.

"Ayron? Do you have family?" Eric shared a look with Tag.

"No, I don't. I just lost my dad a few months ago. Mom went a couple of years before that. I have no siblings." She blinked back tears. "It's so lonely, you know."

"Not any more, love." Tag's hand tightened on hers. "You have me and a large family of officers and their families. You'll be tired of people."

Eric laughed. "That you may well be. But we will support you and Tag, that's a given. Tag, walk out with me. I need to get moving."

Tag stood on the front porch after Eric had walked away, not sure how to proceed. Eric had asked questions that he had no answers for. He sighed as he heard footsteps behind him and Ayron appeared beside him. Without thinking, he reached to wrap an arm around her and draw her close to him.

"Tag?" He could hear the questions in her voice.

"It's okay, Ayron. Eric said that he would have Ella come by. She's about our age and one of the best detectives we have. She'll dig until she finds answers."

"But we don't know how long it will be before those men appear, do we?" Ayron shivered in sudden fear. "But what do we do?"

"What do you mean? What do we do?"

"Us? They will think of us as a couple and expect us to do things together. We're not a couple."

Tag hugged her tighter, finally feeling her return his hug. "We go forward as a couple, love, for now. Then, we'll take when this is all over. We'll learn about one another, our wishes, wants, dreams. We seek for answers. God is here in all this. That is a promise we will cling to. He brought us together for a reason." Tag already knew that Ayron had his heart. He just couldn't tell her that.

"You really believe that? Thank God that you do. I was so worried that you weren't a believer."

Chapter 4

Turning in a circle in his backyard, Tag sighed. Yard work was waiting to be done, but he just didn't want to do that. Ella was due out in a couple of hours, or so she had said when she called. He could hear the questions in her voice and knew the conversation would be a difficult one. He didn't see Ayron watching from the back porch and then moving into his space.

"Tag?" Ayron waited until he stopped his circle, his hand reaching for hers without him thinking about it.

"Ayron? Ella will be out soon, but I need to do some work out here."

"So I see." Ayron moved away from him, heading for the garage. "I'll do the trimming if you do the mowing. Dad and I used to work together."

"Ayron? What about your home? I don't even know where you're from?"

"Up north. It's a small town called Lakeside." She turned when he didn't speak. "Is that a problem?"

Tag approached her, a grin on her face. "Not at all. I have friends who live in the nearby town. Or outside rather."

"You do? I need to go back there at some point." She chewed at her lip. "I need to speak with Dad's lawyer, only I don't trust him."

"Any particular reason why?" Tag pushed the lawnmower from the garage and then headed back for the trimmer. "It's cordless, Ayron. A lot easier to handle."

"Cordless? Dad was looking at getting one but never had a chance." She studied it closely. "The lawyer? I don't think Dad trusted him too much lately. Just a feeling or impression that I have. But I need to go back over Dad's estate."

"Is there a lot?" Tag's arm wrapped around her and she leaned into him.

"No, not really. The house. Some investments." She shot him a look. "I wonder if that's what the problem is."

"Did the men say or ask you anything?"

Ayron shook her head. "Not a thing. They just appeared two weeks ago, made me go with them, even though I fought them, and then drove around for a week until they appeared here. But why here? And why you?"

Ella watched the couple as they walked towards her from the back of the yard. She nodded. Eric was right. They are a couple whether they agreed to that or not. What is the story behind it all? He didn't have a sense of what it was, and that was unusual for him.

Tag grinned at Ella as he neared her. "You're here, Ella, and early. We just finished the yard work."

Ella grinned in response. "And it looks great. Your yard always does. Are you planning of replacing any of the plants?"

"I have no idea. That is something Ayron can work on." He grinned down at her look of surprise. "You can, love. I haven't done much with that, just leaving what was here."

"Hi, Ayron. I'm Ella, the detective who Eric has asked to speak with you both. Did I pronounce your name right?"

"You did. Mom and Dad wanted something different. Some days, I wish they had chosen something like Ann."

"But just plain Ann would not suit you." Ella linked an arm with Ayron. "So tell me. You have coffee and tea?"

"We do. Both in fact. Someone named Stephen did some shopping. I think he bought just about one of everything."

Tag grinned as Ella laughed. "He would do just that, not knowing what you would like. But let's find our beverages and then can we sit out here on the back deck? Tag, it looks so inviting."

"It is, and I searched it earlier today. Nothing there."

Ayron spun to stare at him and he sighed.

"I looked for listening devices, microphones, cameras, anything that could monitor us." He reached to hug Ayron, finding her returning his hug. "We need to do that, Ayron. They know where we live."

"And how?"

"That I don't know. But you can be sure that somehow they have discovered that. Maybe following us from the hospital."

"They would do that?" Ayron rested her hand on the kettle before she lifted it to make her tea and then reached for mugs for coffee for Ella and Tag.

"They would, Ayron." Ella took her coffee with a quiet word of thanks. "Tag, you'll need to do that on a daily basis."

Ella reached for her notepad and then studied both Tag and Ayron.

"Okay, Ayron. Let's start with you, seeing you're the one who started it all." She held up a hand as Ayron went to protest. "By that I mean, you're the one who was abducted, were you not, first?"

Ayron nodded. "I was. And I don't get why. I was at home, trying to sort through Dad's stuff in the garage when I heard a little sound and spun. Two of the men stood there. One reached for my wrist and dragged me outside with him. I fought him. I did manage to get away and back into the garage, but before I could get the door down, he was back. This time, he just picked me up and carried me out. I was screaming and shoving at him, but no one came to help. I don't know if it was reported or not. Anyway, they drove me around the province for a number of days, ending up in this area the day before Tag was taken.

"I managed to escape them and was running for safety when I saw the police car. I approached it, Tag got out, and then they were there. Tag was on the ground before he could even react. He was

---

27

disoriented when he was pulled to his feet, his belt and radio removed and thrown into the car. They made him remove his shirt." She turned to stare at Tag. "They didn't take your phone. Why not?"

"That's what I don't understand. Why not take it? Unless they knew that I wouldn't be able to use it. When we were locked up separately, I did pull it out but the signal wasn't there. They must have blocked it in some way." Tag turned to Ella. "Now, you need to go over your information with us."

"I do. Ayron, you're not from this area. I have what you gave in your statement to Eric. But why you? And why here?"

"That's what Tag and I were talking about." Ayron sighed. "I need to go back to my home and I'm not sure that I want to do that. It's not home any more. It hasn't been since my parents passed away."

"No, your home is here, with Tag." Ella didn't look up from her notes so missed the look of surprise and then acceptance that crossed Ayron's face.

Chapter 5

Two days later, Tag stood in the centre of his front yard, staring at the house. Something was off and he just wasn't sure what. He sighed to himself. He just didn't feel like he should, the effects of his rough treatment still being felt. Stephen had been around that morning, startling Ayron as he appeared in his uniform, ready to go on duty. She hadn't said anything, Tag noted, but she seemed to withdraw. How did he reach through to her? She was building a wall around herself, and he needed her not to do just that.

Ayron stood herself on the front porch, the mail that she had retrieved from the box in her hands. She stared down at the letter on the top, recognizing the lawyer as the one her father had used. But she was puzzled. How did he know her married name? And how on earth did he know her address? He shouldn't. Jumping as she felt Tag's arm come around her, she froze for a moment, surprise doing that to her.

"Ayron? What's wrong?"

She lifted the letter. "This. It's from Dad's lawyer. But how did he know my married name and how did he know my new address? I have not been in touch with him."

Tag stared at her and then reached for the letter. "He shouldn't have. I don't like this, Ayron. In the house with you for a moment. I need to call Ella."

———

"But you were puzzled by something?" Ayron dug in her heels, not moving from the porch.

"There is something different out here, and I just can't place what it is." Tag sighed as he studied her face. She was not going to go into the house, that was obvious. "All right, we'll look around. Does that help?" He followed her down the steps, watching with amusement as she studied the house and then the gardens.

Ayron shrugged "I guess. Tag, do you have family?"

Tag paused, a hand rubbing down his face. "I do. A brother who is married with a little boy. Why?"

"No parents?"

"Mom and Dad are still alive and live near here. I'll take you to meet them tomorrow. They have been away. Why?" Tag searched her face, a frown on his, not sure what she was asking. "They had all been away on vacation. I wouldn't let them come home. Dad flew in when I was first hospitalized but had to leave the next day. That's why I haven't taken you to see them."

"They'll blame me. I just know that." Distress coloured Ayron's face and her voice even as she moved away, her eyes on the garden in the front under the living room window. "Tag? What's this?"

Tag's hand stopped her from touching the object. "I think that you just found what puzzled me. That is not a solar light or an ornament. Not an ordinary one. This is what I was seeing without knowing that. Thank you, Ayron. Now, into the house. I have to call it in."

Ayron refused to move, her eyes on the window. "Tag? Is that what they're doing? Placing things around to track us?"

"I am sure they are. And I need to let Ella know about that letter from the lawyer. If it's okay with you, then we'll have her open it."

Ayron shook her head and then almost ran for the house, the door closing quietly behind her. Tag stood and watched, shocked in some ways at how she had reacted, his hands on the top of his head. He turned as he heard his name called. His next-door neighbour, Paul, walked towards him.

"Tag? How are you? I heard tell you've been having an adventure." Paul watched him closely, knowing Tag from their church as well.

"I have been, Paul, and I can tell you that it's no fun."

"No, I don't expect that it has been." He studied the house. "Who's the lady?"

Tag stared at him before his eyes slid closed. "It's a long story, Paul. That's Ayron, my wife." He didn't see the startled look that Paul shot at him. "Long story short? I know that you'll keep my confidence but as the church board chair, I'll need you to talk to the board. We were both kidnapped. I chose to marry Ayron to save her life. They had threatened to kill her unless I did. I couldn't do anything else." Tag knew that he was almost pleading for Paul to understand.

Paul felt Tag jump as he rested his hand on the younger man's shoulder.

—

"We understand, Tag. Your Dad called me and asked that I speak with the board. We plan on speaking with the congregation on Sunday, if we have your permission."

Tag shrugged even as his hand reached for Ayron's, who had approached and hesitated to come close.

"Paul, this is my bride, Ayron. Ayron, my love, this is Paul Smith, our next-door neighbour, but also our church board chair. Dad somehow figured out that I tried to protect you, but not how. Paul has spoken with the church board with what little information Dad was able to provide. We need to sit down with him over the next couple of days. He'll talk with the board and then approach the church."

Ayron shot a look of horror at first Tag and then Paul, finding Paul watching her closely, a smile on his face.

"We don't bite, Ayron. That we don't. In fact, you will be welcomed gladly as Tag's helpmeet."

Ayron shook her head, fear running through her as well as an emotion that she had never expected to feel. She didn't want to leave Tag, ever, but knew that she had to, at some point. She was bringing danger to him.

"It's just temporary. I mean, once we find who is responsible and why, we go our separate ways." Ayron turned as she heard a car door shut and almost ran towards Ella.

"That's not happening, is it, Tag?" Paul's hand rested lightly on Tag's shoulder. "When you're up to it in the next day or so, come over for a meal. Suzy will be glad to meet your lady." He nodded to where Ella and Ayron stood talking at the front of the house, Ayron pointing at the object that they had found. "You're not letting her go and she's not walking away. Not ever."

Chapter 6

Wandering the house late that night, just unable to settle down, Tag rubbed at his forehead with a thumb and index finger. He had not been expecting Paul to approach him as he had, nor to hear that his father had reached out to the board. Just what all had his father said, he wondered. He turned as he heard a slight sound, heading for Ayron, finding her sitting on the side of her bed, her hands covering her face. With an inaudible sound, he was beside her, his arms wrapped around her, a prayer rising for her.

Ayron jumped as she felt Tag's touch and then leaned into it. She could grow to like this, she thought, and mentally shook her head. She was too dangerous, she thought. *I need to leave and I just don't know how to do that very deed.* Tag's prayer finally caught at her ear and she listened to his words, the verses that he quoted, how he begged for safety for her, that she would be hidden in the hollow of God's hand and protected.

Tag felt when she relaxed and tilted his head to look down at her, seeing that she had fallen asleep. He moved to lay her down and tuck a blanket around her before he stood, his eyes on the wall in front of him, and then moved from there, heading for his office. He hurt physically, but emotionally, he was hurting even more, hurting for his young bride. Tag squinted at the clock and then headed for the kitchen instead. He needed coffee and lots of it. He had

---

research to do. And just maybe tomorrow, after he had taken Ayron over and introduced her to his family, he would head north and catch up with Evan. Evan and Flannery would help him, that he knew, as would Dooley, an officer that he had gotten to know well from that force, and Evan's neighbours, Eunice, another officer, and Everett, a retired paramedic.

His head rising at a slight sound, Tag rose from his desk. He had finally given up on the research, not finding what he knew he needed to find. His thoughts had gone back to the afternoon before and Ella's conversation with them.

Ayron had been adamant that she wanted nothing to do with the lawyer and could not understand just how he had her married name and address. She had not been in touch with him, so just who had done that? Tag had shared a look with Ella who had nodded. They were on the same wavelength, Tag thought, that their kidnappers had done that and to somehow be connected with the lawyer.

The crime scene tech had been around, gathering what little evidence that he could. Jay had simply shaken his head when Tag had approached him.

Ella had opened the letter from the lawyer, scanning it before her eye lifted to Ayron, a puzzled look on her face.

"Ayron? This was your father's lawyer?"

"It was. I mean, I think he was. Dad had talked about moving his files to some other lawyer after Mom passed away, but I am not sure if he did."

"And how did your mother die?" Ella's notepad was out, her pen poised over it to jot down her notes.

"A heart attack. She had had heart disease since she was young. It wasn't her first heart attack but she was alone when it happened. The medical examiner said that there wouldn't have been anything anyone could have done even if she had had treatment right away."

"Given what you're going through, I would like to speak with the medical examiner. Were the police involved?"

"They were. Dad called in the paramedics when he found her and they called in the police." Ayron shuddered at the memory before she frowned. "You know, Dad never talked much about it but I could see a question on his face at times, as if he was puzzled. I asked him one time if Mom's heart was that bad and he just shrugged and said he didn't think so."

Tag's arm wrapped around Ayron at that point.

"Let Ella work her way through this, my love. We can do it in an official manner, seeing as it is likely related to what we are going through."

Ayron's head shot around at that point, a frown on her face.

"I don't see that."

"What Tag is saying, Ayron, is that we need to look at you and your family. To determine if there is something there as to the reason you were kidnapped and threatened with death." Ella's gaze was compassionate as she handed Tag the letter.

His eyes on Ayron for a moment, Tag hesitated to read the letter. His eyes dropped at last to it and he froze before he looked up at Ella, who nodded.

"Ayron? This is not from your lawyer."

"It's not? It has his envelope." She leaned against him as she read it. "Little brutal, aren't they? And yes, it is from the law firm. That's his son, and his son does nothing without his father's approval or direction. So, if he has sent that letter, his father would likely have dictated it." She raised her eyes, a thoughtful look on her face. "But I don't have anything that they want. What is it that they are really after?"

"I think that Tag and you will need to make a trip there. But not on your own." Ella looked over at Tag as he made a sound. "Tag?"

"It's near where Evan and Flannery live. In fact, I think their police force helps to cover that small town at times. I can ask for Dooley or Eunice to go with us."

"And they would be?"

"Friends but also police officers in Evan's town."

The agreement had been reached that at some point in the next few days Tag and Ayron would head that way. Ella made a note to herself to speak with Eric and see who they could send. That is, if Tag let them know when he was heading that way.

Tag's thoughts came back to the present time and he squinted as he looked at the clock. It was that late in the morning? He frowned as he headed for the

—

door, opening to find his parents and brother standing there, his father's finger reaching for the doorbell once more.

Chapter 7

Thurlow Rafferty took one look at his son, seeing the ravages that the stress and pain had etched into Tag's face and just reached to draw him into a father hug. Meg shared a look with their youngest son, Tully, and then reached for Tag, her mother arms cradling her oldest son as she had when he had been hurt as a child. Tag didn't even attempt to hide his emotions as his father moved them away from the door and to the kitchen. Tully simply reached for the coffee pot, raising it to stare at the sludge on the bottom before he looked at his brother.

Turning as he heard a faint sound, Thurlow stared at the young woman who had stopped in the kitchen doorway, sudden fright on her face, before she moved towards Tag. Tag stepped away from his mother's arm and reached for Ayron, hugging her to him even as his eyes found his father.

"Mom, Dad, Tully? Can we sit? This will take a while." He pulled out a chair, shoved Ayron down in it even as she frowned at him, and then sat himself, his hand reaching for hers.

"Tag? What is going on?" Meg stared between the young couple, seeing the flushing and embarrassment on Ayron's face and the distress on Tag.

Tag accepted the mug of coffee handed him by Tully with a quiet word of thanks before he was on

—

his feet, making the tea that he knew Ayron would want. He was back on his chair, his hand reaching for hers, tightening on it as she tried to pull it away.

"Mom, Dad, Tully? This is hard." His eyes never left Ayron's face. "This is Ayron. She is my bride." His words stopped at the shocked voices that arose around him. His hand went up. "I know. I wasn't dating, had no desire to. You know that I was taken captive, kidnapped, whatever you want to call it about ten days or so. I am told, Dad, that you were back for overnight during the time I was in the hospital. I don't remember that."

"I was, son. I heard the muttering that you were doing. I wondered."

"Paul talked to me. Said that you had reached out to him." Tag searched his father's face.

"I did, son. I felt I had to. I didn't have a lot of information, other than that you were worried about a young lady. I assume that it was Ayron?"

"It was, Dad. I had parked for my break and saw Ayron running towards me. I got out to speak with her and help her. Before I could, two trucks had approached. I was on the ground before I could do or say anything. My utility belt and radio? I was forced to leave them in the car, as well as my uniform shirt. They threatened Ayron at that point, just why I wasn't sure. We were taken to a house and kept there. A couple of hours later, the men reappeared. We were moved to a room where we were together. They demanded that I marry Ayron. I refused and with each refusal was beaten. They threatened to kill her, Dad, unless I did marry her. I couldn't do anything else."

—

His family heard the distress in his voice, the reality of what he had faced driven home to them by the looks on the young couple's faces.

"No, I know that you would not want that." Thurlow's heart raised in prayer for them. "They had a minister or a justice of the peace?"

"A minister. He tried to refuse but faced the same scenario. Ayron would be killed unless he performed the wedding. We need to find him and make sure that he gets help."

"We'll look after that, son. The marriage was registered?"

Tag nodded. "Apparently so. Ella searched that for us. It was registered right away, she said. This is so unfair to Ayron."

Tully had risen to find paper and a pen and was jotting notes, a thoughtful look on his face.

"Why?" His question had Tag's head turning towards him.

"That's what we don't get, Tully. The thing of it is that Ayron received a letter from her father's lawyer yesterday. In her married name. And addressed to here. She has not been in touch with them to make any changes. Ella was reaching out to the police in her town. There are also questions about her mother's death."

"Your parents are both gone, Ayron?" Meg reached for Ayron's hand, hers warming the coldness of Ayron's.

"They are. Mom two years ago. Dad just a few months ago." Ayron frowned. "We didn't have a lot.

—

41

Dad worked in construction, Mom stayed home. They didn't have a lot of savings or investments. Just a few. I don't understand why."

Thurlow nodded, his mind racing as to possibilities. He was a private investigator and his mind was already racing as to what and where and why. "I can start an investigation, Ayron, with your permission. I am an investigator. We just need to get all the information from you that we can."

Tag looked around as he heard the doorbell and grinned to himself at Ayron's muttered comment about her home being a train station. Meg was on her feet, heading for the door, returning in a moment with Eric. Eric shook his head slightly at Tag's questioning look. Tag sighed. Eric was here for a reason and he just knew that he wouldn't like it.

Ayron rose, moving away from them all, Tag on his feet watching him. His mother's hand stopped his forward movement and then she moved after the younger woman.

Meg watched Ayron closely as she paced Tag's home office before she moved towards her. Ayron spun, fear on her face for a moment.

"Ayron? What can I do for you?" Meg's eyes studied her intently, seeing the fear that Ayron was trying so desperately to hide.

"Keep Tag away from me. They almost killed him when they did that to him. And I don't know why." Ayron blinked at the tears. "I just don't know why."

Chapter 8

Watching as his family drove away, Tag sighed. The day had not gone as he had hoped. His family had welcomed Ayron, accepting her into their midst, but he could sense the hesitation that she felt. How did he reach her, Lord? How did he make her understand that he would choose no other lady to share his life? That God had brought them together and he would not walk away from her ever. Eric had remained behind, knowing that he needed to speak with Tag and also Ayron, if only he could stop that lady from disappearing.

Ayron approached Eric, a question on her face. She was comfortable with him, she thought, just not Tag's family. Not that that made much sense. She just didn't understand that she was afraid for them as well, that his family had been threatened. Ayron had buried that deep inside her.

"Eric? You wanted to speak with us?"

"I do, Ayron. Just for a bit. How are you now?" Eric watched with compassion as she shrugged.

"I really don't know, Eric. How am I to feel?" She kept the bite from the words that she so wanted to include.

"Afraid. Terrified. Fearful for Tag and his family and friends. About like that?" Eric smiled at her.

"Just about like that." Ayron jumped as Tag's arm came around her. "Tag?"

"Ayron?" He mimicked her tone of voice, a small smile on his face. "Eric needs to speak with us?"

"I do, Tag, but first, have you two eaten yet today? I know you well, Tag. You would have been working all night, researching."

"I was." He shook his head at Eric. "I have sandwich stuff."

"Sandwich stuff works. Ayron, let's me serve you. You're still not steady on your feet."

Ayron glared at Eric. "I am so. Steady on my feet, that is. It's just this, whatever this is, that has me unsteady."

Eric grinned, knowing that Ayron was doing that on purpose, trying to lighten the air around them. "I am sure it is. Tag, lead on to the kitchen. We eat. We pray. We talk. Then, we plan."

An hour later, Eric reached for the folder that he had dropped on the counter. He had hesitated at first when Ella had approached him, thinking that she should be the one to speak with Tag. She had shaken her head, stated that she didn't know how that information related to what they were going through, and seeing that Eric was the supervising officer and would need to know what was going on with Tag and when he would be able to return to work, he needed to be the one speaking with Tag.

"Eric? You look troubled." Tag's hands wrapped around his mug, his eyes on Ayron. Ayron was refusing to look at either man, her eyes on her clasped hands.

"I am. Ella approached me with some information and neither one of us is sure how it applies to either one of you or to what you just went through." He opened the folder, closed it, sighed, and then shoved it across the table. "Take a look at this, both of us, and then talk to me."

Tag shared a look with Ayron, a frown in place for a moment at the look in her eyes, a look that gave him hope that his feelings were reciprocated. He flipped open the folder, staring at the photo.

Ayron leaned closer, a finger touching it.

"Who is this? It looks like Dad, but it's not. He was an only child of an only child of an only child."

"That we are not sure of, Ayron. You do not know him?" Eric's voice brought her head up to stare at him.

Shaking her head, she looked back at the man. "No, I don't. I have no idea who it is. I know that it's said we all have a double, but this can't be right." She moved the photo aside, to read the paperwork underneath. "A distant relative? That's bizarre. Both Mom and Dad said they had no contact with any relatives. Once their parents were gone, they didn't have anyone to contact. Mom was an only child, with just a sister on her side. Her sister is gone as well, but she never married, had no children."

"For the record then, Ayron, you deny knowing this person and are unfamiliar with anything about him?"

—

45

"I am. Tag? Do you know him?"

Tag nodded his head, his eyes on Ayron. "Unfortunately, I do. He was there, Ayron. He kept himself behind you at all times, but he must be one of the bosses to the men. He was directing them."

"He was? And you're just telling me now?" Ayron's anger flared and then subsided. "I'm sorry. I know that things can get buried when we go through trauma." Her voice paused, as she sat staring past Eric, a puzzled look on her face. "Eric? Is there any way to find out about the paramedics who responded to the call for Mom? I felt at the time that something was off."

"We are looking into them already as well as anyone else that Ella can think of." Eric sipped at his mug of cold coffee, not even realizing that it had grown cold. "I think that you will need to make a trip up there soon."

"That's our plan. Dad had offered to go with us."

"That might be a good idea." Eric stood, reaching to set his mug in the sink. "One of us should like to go with you."

Ayron shook her head. "I'm not sure on that. It's putting more people at risk."

"They want to do that for you, Ayron. Tag is well thought of among his fellow officers. And yes, they know that you two are married. The chief felt that they should be told." He smiled at her, seeing her shock and uncertainty on her face. "You are welcomed, Ayron, as a member of our family."

46

"I am? And just what family?" Ayron was on her feet, running for the back door, closing it quickly behind her.

Tag stood, a large sigh drawn from him. "I need to stop her from doing that. Running."

"You do, and good luck doing just that. She'll continue to run. Only you're not letting her go, are you, Tag?" Eric walked away, leaving Tag staring after him.

Chapter 9

Two days later, Ayron stared at the cabin or cottage or whatever you wanted to call in that Tag had stopped near. She hadn't spoken much to him over the last two days, trying to come to terms with her parents' death once more. That had been difficult to do, and she wasn't even sure if she could. Ella had called, just to talk, she said, not about what they were going through, but just as a friend. Ayron had appreciated that. Any friends that she had had? They had long since disappeared, and she was lonely. She had been adamant that she would not go to church with Tag, and he had simply hugged her, agreed, and then found his Bible to spend time in God's Word with her. He had asked her if she had her Bible and she had shaken her head, quietly stating that she didn't and that she had no idea where it was. Did he?

Tag watched the emotions crossing his lady's face and sighed. Ayron was not making it easy for him, not at all. He had brought her north to his friend, Evan's home, just to talk and then they planned on heading over to her own home. Only, he suddenly felt that was a bad idea. That Ayron would be in grave danger, and he wanted to avoid that at all costs.

"Why are we here?" Ayron refused to look at Tag.

"This is my friend, Evan's place. He was an officer until he quit the force a few months ago. He and his wife, Flannery, went through what we term as an adventure. They have offered to help us, if we wish them to. I would just like to see them. If you don't wish to, we will leave."

Staring at him, a horrified look on her face, Ayron sputtered to get her words out.

"You can't just drive away. They'll have seen you. It would be really rude to do that." She looked past him, out of his window, at the lady about her own age, she thought, who approached. "Tag?"

"Yes?" He turned as he heard Flannery's voice calling to him. He was out of the car, hugging her, and then running around to open Ayron's door, a hand held out for her.

Ayron stared at his hand, at him, and then at Flannery as she stood near the front of the car, a welcoming smile on her face.

"It's okay, Ayron. You will not be judged. Not by Flannery. Not by Evan. Not by my friends here." He looked up as he heard voices. "And here are Evan and Dooley."

Two hours later, Tag watched as Ayron worked with Flannery in the kitchen, preparing a meal for them all, before he turned at Evan's voice.

"Tag? What's going on? You didn't respond for a week to any messages, and then you show up here, married?" Evan shared a look with Dooley, who simply shook his head.

"I'm not sure what all is going on. I was abducted while on duty and trying to help Ayron. We were forced to marry in order to keep her alive. They

—

49

threatened to kill her in front of me. I took a beating before I agreed. We're working on that, Eric and Ella as well."

"Ella?" Evan frowned for a moment. He had not gotten to know Ella well but he had always had a hesitation about her. "Eric's okay with that?"

"He is. You're not sure on Ella?" Tag had picked up on that.

"No, I'm not. I don't know here but there were rumblings on the street about her."

Tag sighed, his head dropping. "She's been talking with Ayron every day. Not that Ayron will say much. She's not even talking to me." His eyes lifted to Ayron, finding her watching him. "We'll talk more, Evan. Dooley, what do you know of this man?" Tag named the lawyer, watching Dooley closely.

Dooley stared at him. "He's involved? How?"

"He was my father's lawyer. Do you know him?" Ayron had approached, Flannery following her. She slipped under the arm that Tag had raised to draw her close to him.

"I do. We've had complaints about him, which I can't discuss. But he is under investigation, not just by us."

"What did he do?" Flannery beckoned them to the table and waited until they had all be seated and a blessing asked on their meal before she repeated her question.

Dooley thought through what he could say to them. There was not a lot that he could, unfortunately.

He would have their chief reach out to Eric, he decided, if Eric had not contacted their force.

"What I can say is that they are rumours, and just rumours at this point, that he is involved in white-collar crime and forgery."

"Forgery?" Ayron sat back. "That makes sense, then."

"What does?" Tag's hand reached for hers.

"There were documents that I didn't understand in Dad's paperwork. I had set them aside, locked into the safe, until I could talk with him. Only, I never did." Her eyes were huge as she looked around. "Did he do that?"

"It's possible." Evan looked at the clock. "How be we head over there in the morning? Dooley, are you on duty?"

"No, I'm not but even if I were, I would be able to go with you. The chief would agree to that." Dooley watched Ayron closely before he looked over at Tag, finding Tag watching her with his heart on his face. He shook his head at Evan, knowing that Evan had been the same with Flannery. What was it with these two? He had found his own lady without an adventure. But these two? They couldn't seem to do just that. They had to come to the rescue, and that could well mean their lives, now didn't it? Evan had survived. But the question was, would Tag? That Dooley was not sure of.

Evan walked out with Dooley, his eyes turning back to the cabin.

"Dooley? What didn't you say?"

—

51

Dooley shrugged. "There's not much that I can say, Evan. You know how it goes. You'll be talking with Eunice?"

"We will. Tag said that they were heading into town to the B&B for tonight. We'll get together with Eunice and Everett tomorrow."

Chapter 10

Ayron stood mid-morning the next day, her hand tight in Tag's, as she stared at her home. A puzzled look crossed her face, causing Tag's gaze to shift between her and the house before he looked at Evan. Evan shrugged, his own eyes going back to Ayron.

"Ayron?" Flannery spoke from beside her. "Something's off about the house?"

"There is. It seems different than it did two weeks or so ago. But what?" She moved to step forward, tugging at her hand as Tag stopped her.

"Ayron, wait. First, we need to bathe you and this situation in prayer. Then, I think we'll ask the local force to go through your home before you do. If you're sensing something, then we must."

Tag walked towards the responding officer, Dooley keeping pace with him, Evan staying with the two ladies as they waited near the cars. He reached to shake the officer's hand.

"Brownie? I didn't know you were on this force. I knew that you had moved on."

"I had, Tag. I didn't expect to see you here. What's the story?" Brownie's keen eyes studied Tag before he looked past him at the other three. "Ayron's here? How do you know her? We've been trying to find her, but haven't been able to. Her phone goes right to voice mail."

"A long story, Brownie, but the short version? We were both kidnapped, I married her to save her from being killed, and we suspect that her lawyer and his son are somehow involved."

Brownie stared at Tag and then nodded. "That makes sense. Those are the rumours that we've been hearing about him being involved in crime. He denies it, but we think he is protesting too much. His son has disappeared and we hear that he headed your way." He walked towards Ayron.

"Ayron? You're okay?" He grinned at her disgruntled look.

"Okay? That's relative, Brownie. Can we go in?"

"Let me have your keys. Dooley and I will head through and then come back for you." He held up a hand at her protest. "We've been trying to reach you, Ayron. Your neighbours have reported men hanging around here and a surveyor has been around as well."

"A surveyor? What?"

"That's what we'll look into. Usually, that is done if the house is being sold, isn't it?" Tag wrapped Ayron into his arms.

"Usually." Brownie took her keys and moved away, Dooley keeping step with him.

"Ayron?" Flannery's soft voice brought Ayron back to the present and her eyes to Flannery.

"Flannery? I'm too dangerous for you to be around. You need to leave."

Flannery just grinned even as Evan laughed. "Didn't I tell you my story? I was on the streets for years, had drug lords after me, and then disappeared for a week or so." She reached to hug Ayron and then watched as Brownie and Dooley stood talking on the front porch of the house before they walked around the yard.

Evan and Tag shared a look. Something had been found, that much the two men had figured out. Just what, they were not sure of.

Brownie approached Ayron slowly, trying to sort through his thoughts. He had placed a call for the crime scene techs to come out after speaking with his supervisor. Ayron would not be going through her home any time soon. He paused, his phone in his hand, ready to show her the pictures that he had taken.

"Brownie? What is wrong? Can I go in?" Ayron stepped forward, ready to head for her home, before Tag's hand stopped her. "Tag? What is going on?" She began to shake, her emotions overcoming her for the moment.

"I'm sorry, Ayron. You can't. I have some pictures to show you and I have a team coming out to go through your home." He shared a look with Tag, who nodded.

"What do you mean? Of course, I can. Tag?" Ayron spun to him, seeing the compassionate look on his face. "Tag? I want to go in there!" She was becoming more agitated as the moments passed.

—

"Ayron, my love. Let's see what Brownie has to show us. Then, we'll know why." He reached for Brownie's phone, a prayer raising for his bride.

Ayron stared at Tag and then down at the phone, a hand covering her mouth as she stared at the photos that Tag was scrolling through.

"This isn't right. That's not our furnishings. Where are they?" She looked up, shock on her face. "What did he do?"

"That's what we're now looking at. I have one of the detectives heading his way and then searching for a storage unit that would hold your items."

Tag nodded his thanks even as he watched the teams moving in. He sighed. This is not what he had expected. He felt Evan touch his arm and then nod towards Dooley. Tag and Evan moved away, heading for Dooley.

"Dooley? What didn't Brownie say?" Tag went right to the point.

"Her home is stripped of all her belongings. It has been repainted. We found paperwork on the kitchen counter from a real estate agent and a signed sales agreement. We know Ayron didn't sign it, but it has a signature on it purporting to be hers." He looked around as he heard a car stop abruptly and then raised voices. He sighed. "And I would imagine these are the new owners."

Chapter 11

Tag moved as quickly as he could, an arm around Ayron as she stared in horror at the couple standing in front of her, the man's voice loud and angry as he demanded to know why the police were in his new house.

Brownie moved to stand between Ayron and the man, a hand raised.

"There are irregularities here. This house has been sold fraudulently. This is the owner behind me. She never agreed to sell her house."

"Of course she did." The man peered around Brownie. "No, she's not the owner. It was an older lady. Arrest her." His finger stabbed towards Ayron, who continued to stare at him in horror, not seeing the neighbours gathering on their lawns to watch the commotion.

"No, she didn't. You spoke with a lawyer?" Brownie's keen eyes watched the man closely.

"We did. He had us sign the paperwork. Why? I still want that woman arrested for trespassing." He didn't see the officer who had approached behind him, a hand on his weapon as he paused.

"First, there will be no arrests for trespassing. She is still legally the owner. We saw the paperwork, and she has denied signing off anything. In fact, the

57

date you signed it? She was in a town hundreds of miles from here. We have proof of that." Brownie pointed to their car. "You will step back there with the officer standing behind you."

The man blustered and threatened before he charged at Ayron. The officer tackled him and took him down, handcuffs slapped on his wrists before he was hauled to his feet and directed to the patrol vehicle and shoved inside. His wife stalked after him, threats of lawsuits tumbling from her mouth.

Ayron shrank back again Tag even as Evan and Dooley moved in front of the pair, Flannery flanking Tag, ready to fight for her new friend if necessary. Brownie shook his head and then moved off to speak with the crime scene tech, spinning to stare at the man.

Tag moved towards him, Ayron's hand tight in his.

"Brownie? What's up? This is not normal."

"No, it's not. Sally here says that it looks as if they have moved in. But your keys still work, Ayron." He was puzzled. "Let's walk you through the house. Did you have a safe, by chance?"

"I do. There are documents in there that we need. This is an ancestral home and cannot be sold. The lawyer would have been aware of that." She headed after Brownie, ignoring the shouts from behind her. Evan and Dooley moved behind them, Flannery between the two men.

Ayron stopped just inside the door, her hand covering her mouth as she tried to control her emotions. What had happened in here? There were a lot of changes in the last two weeks or so, she thought. Numbed with shock, she moved forward, her hand in Tag's as she searched the rooms on the main floor, then climbed the staircase to the second floor. She stood in the doorway to her room, not able to cross the threshold and enter it.

Tag watched her closely, seeing her emotions fluctuating as she moved through her childhood home. He looked over at Brownie, who shook his head.

"Ayron?"

"Tag, what did they do?" She spun and headed for the master bedroom, sliding to a stop as she stared at the furniture. "This is so wrong." She headed for the walk-in closet, finding the panel that she needed to move aside, and then spun the dial on the safe, pulling it open. She breathed a sigh of relief as she found the paperwork that her father had left there. Ayron removed it, finding Tag's hands there to take it from her.

Brownie turned back to them, his eyes on the open safe.

"No one would have known about it?"

"I don't think so. Dad never talked about it." Ayron looked devastated as she stared back into her parents' room. "Who did this, Brownie?

"The lawyer. We have brought him in for questioning." He turned as an officer approached him and walked away, his eyes searching out the window, before he walked back to them. "We need to leave, Ayron and Tag. Don't worry. An officer has been assigned to stay here. The chief wants that."

59

Tag stood later that afternoon, watching Ayron as she stood near the lake. Evan had insisted that they return to his home, knowing that Tag wanted to keep Ayron safe and wasn't sure how to do that where he was. Ayron had handed Evan the papers, told him to go through them, and talk to her later.

Evan approached Tag, the paperwork in his hand.

"Tag? Her father was very thorough. Did she know that he suspected something?"

"I am not sure. She mentioned something but I don't know her well enough to read her." Tag sighed. "This is not how I planned this."

"I know. It never works out that way. Listen, Dooley said that he'd be back later. He had some investigation to do."

"That's what he said." Tag sighed as his phone chimed and he looked at it. "Ella. And I am really not sure about her."

"Ella?" Evan's face paled. "She's named in here. She's a niece to the lawyer. Did you know that?"

Tag stared at him, startled. "No, I didn't. Oh, man, what did we do?" His phone was out and he sent a text message off to Eric, letting him know that Ella had to be taken off their case and why. He knew Eric would call him shortly.

"Did you tell her anything about her?"

"No, come to think of it, we didn't. We did to Eric so he may have. This just gets worse and worse.

She's hurting in more ways than one, Evan. How do I help her?"

"Leave her with God, my friend. Treat her like the treasure that she is. Pray for her and with her. Study the passages of protection and hope that we all know so well."

"That's about all I can do."

"Your heart's involved, isn't it?" Evan's hand went up. "No, don't talk to me. At some point, you need to talk with Ayron. But neither one of you are there yet."

"No, we're not. I don't know that we ever will be."

Evan grinned. "Flannery and I were like that but we eventually talked and cleared it all up. She's the love of my life, even with how we met."

Chapter 12

Flannery watched Ayron as she moved back towards the cabin, reaching out with a mug of tea for her. She waited as Ayron hesitated before she moved to sit in one of the deck chairs on the dock.

"Flannery? You went through something. How did you ever do it?"

"God. I wasn't sure if He even cared when it all started. Evan assured me that He did. Eunice and Everett did as well. I hated that we went through this but it drew us closer than if we had just met and decided to date."

"I see. I guess that's what happened with Tag and me." Ayron's head went back on the chair. "His father's been around and is starting an investigation for us. I just don't know."

"You're not sure if he should. You want this over and you know it won't be, not for a while."

Ayron sighed. "I know. I am afraid, not just for Tag. For his family and friends. The men who held us? They threatened so many people." She looked over to see Flannery nodding.

"They will do that. They did it with us." Flannery looked up as she felt Evan's hand on her shoulder. "Evan? What can we do that's fun? These two need to forget about this for a while."

Evan grinned down at her. "The lake is calm. We could go out in the canoes."

Flannery snorted even as Evan laughed. "Those are waves, Evan. I keep telling you, waves are dangerous."

Tag began to laugh, remembering how Flannery had teased Evan about the lake before they had married. He explained it to Ayron, who stared at Flannery before she too smiled.

"Yes, waves are dangerous. How dangerous do you want to live?"

Flannery stared at her for a moment and then was on her feet, reaching for her hand.

"Very dangerous. You and I against these two."

Ayron stared at her in turn before she began to laugh.

"You're on."

Tag studied them and then turned to Evan.

"Did that just happen? Were we challenged to something we don't know about?"

Evan was laughing even as he headed for the end of the dock.

"We were. I have to warn you about Flannery. She will see this as a challenge that she intends to win."

"I wasn't aware that we were competing for anything." Tag shook his head. "But she's good for Ayron. Ayron needs this."

Late that night, Tag stood at the window of the bedroom that they had been assigned at the B&B, hearing Ayron moving around quietly behind him. He sighed to himself. Today had not gone as he had expected it to, not at all. That his bride had been devastated at the changes in her home and the fact that someone had tried to sell it had been evident. Tag knew that he had to speak with her. Brownie had called him with an update. And Eric had called, questioning why Tag had sent him that text message.

Ayron stood for a moment, just watching Tag, her thoughts muddled. She tried to pray but didn't feel as it was going very far. Her parents would have reassured her that God was hearing and working even when she didn't feel that He was. Only she didn't think that He was. She wouldn't be going through this if He was. She approached Tag, finding his arm coming out to encircle her and draw her to him, his chin on her head.

Praying for his bride, Tag just stood for a moment after he finished. He had prayed for her to be kept hidden in the cleft of the rock, covered with the Good Lord's hand and that He would protect her in every way. He sighed to himself. Tag knew that he had been around the block too many times, as his mother would say, to realistically expect that.

"Tag? Have you heard from Brownie?" Ayron's voice had hope.

"I have, my love." Tag turned her to the couch in the room, seating her and then himself, his arm tight around her. "I have. He can't find the lawyer or the son."

"That doesn't surprise me. Don't they always disappear?" Ayron sighed, a deep from within her sigh. "What else?"

"Brownie found the storage unit with your belongings. He has a court order to open it and restore them to you. He also has a court order to move out all of the items now in your home. Brownie asked about repainting it all for you and what other changes you want to make."

"He would do that?" She felt Tag's nod. "Okay. I guess we'll need to go back through there. The flooring hasn't been changed. The kitchen is the same, I think. I was in too much shock to really notice."

"Brownie will meet us there tomorrow." Tag rubbed at his forehead. The headache that he had been fighting all day had intensified, one of the side effects of his beating. "And I spoke with Eric."

"I bet that went well."

"Actually, it did. He wasn't aware that Ella was that close to the lawyer. He has removed her and she has agreed to that. She has not had contact with that uncle or cousin since she was tiny, she says. He's verifying that. But Ella did state that when she saw who the lawyer was, she expected this. Everything that she has been investigating is ready for someone else to take over."

Ayron's mouth opened and then closed. She finally shook her head.

"What if that was what he wanted? By sending me that letter? To have her taken off the case, knowing that she was his niece?"

Tag stared at her and then reached for his phone, a message sent to Eric, before he set the phone aside, content to sit and hold his lady.

"Did you have fun today, after all?"

Ayron began to laugh, the sound low in the room. "I did. Flannery is a character. She and Evan are so well suited. Did God do that?"

Chapter 13

Her hand tight in Tag's once more, Ayron stared at her home, not sure if she really wanted to go back through it. It was mid-morning of the next day, and Brownie had tracked them down. All the belongings from the other people had been packed up and moved out. The police force had seen to that overnight, despite the man's vehement protests and threats of a lawsuit. He had not backed down at all even when he was presented with the evidence that it had been a fraudulent deal.

Tag waited, knowing that it would take his bride a while. Brownie stood beside him, Flannery and Evan with them as well. Tag looked behind him as he heard other footsteps and saw Everett and Eunice approaching. Good, he thought. Eunice can help. Then his eyes lifted and he saw his parents and his brother and his wife, his little nephew tight in his father's arms.

"Ayron? When you are ready, we will go in." Brownie waited, knowing that there were patrol officers around. There had been word come in from the streets of the small town that Ayron called her home about a hit being put out on her and also on Tag. Just why that was, no one could verify. Tag had shrugged, commenting that it was always that way. Someone had already tried to kill him and been unsuccessful. Unless and until God said otherwise, he would not die.

Ayron finally nodded, her eyes lifting to Tag who nodded in turn and then turned to look behind him once more.

"Everett? Can you and Dad pray for this? We need this." His hand tightened on Ayron's as she jumped, not realizing so many people had gathered around her.

Tag waited as Brownie unlocked the door, his eyes on Ayron. Ayron drew in a deep breath, hearing footsteps behind her as she entered her home, her eyes searching, a breath of relief wafting through her. This was better. She still felt violated, she thought, that her home has invaded and changed.

"Tag? They've painted?" She moved forward, seeing the rooms freshly painted. "How?"

"Brownie said they had more volunteers than they could really use. Painters. Cleaners. Electricians. Whoever it was that was needed moved through here overnight, to bring it back to almost what you had. They tried to match the colours as best they could. They were able to find the colours by scraping near the trim. Is it close?"

"It is." Ayron turned, searching for Brownie before she moved to hug him, unable to speak for a moment. "Thank you." Her voice was low and broken with her emotions.

"You're welcome." Brownie set her back from himself, his head ducking to see her face. "I guess that we did okay."

"You did. Did you find the lawyer or his son?"

"We found the son. Unfortunately, he can't answer any questions for us." Brownie nodded at the look Tag threw him. "He was a drug user and overdosed. We're not sure if it was deliberate or accidental."

Ayron nodded, her eyes on the wall across from her, a frown on her face. "Likely killed. His father was rumoured to be brutal. I heard that after Dad died." She looked up. "Do we know for sure it was natural for Dad?"

"We're looking into that, Ayron. Our detectives had that thought. You are aware of how well thought of your parents were in town."

She nodded, a bleak look crossing her face before she walked to the wall, feeling it.

"There's something off here, Tag. I'm not sure what." She turned her head, finding Brownie near her. "Was this patched at all?"

"Not that I am aware of. What makes you think that?"

Ayron shrugged. "I just feel that things have been changed, added, are different." She sighed. "But then again, having had what has happened, happen? That could be doing it."

Brownie shared a look with Tag before Tag reached to hug Ayron.

"We'll look around, my love. Right now, I understand there are fellows here to replace everything for you."

"There are?" Ayron looked around him, finally seeing the men and ladies standing there. "Hi!"

"Ayron, these are men and ladies from all the emergency services, your church, and others that are friends. Just let us know where everything goes. It won't take long." Evan turned as he spoke, watching Everett. "Everett? Once again, we need you to bathe this home and this couple in prayer."

Chapter 14

Mid-afternoon that day, Tag quietly shut the front door, his eyes on the hallway. He shook his head at the assistance that they had had, the men and ladies just working away without saying much. He had come to appreciate the parents of the lady he loved, even though he had never met them. The stories and words that he had been told that day helped to fill in that gap. Evan had warned him that they were just heading into one of the worst parts of what they faced. Tag had nodded, taking the envelope that he was handed, wondering at the animal tracks covering it.

Evan had grinned, said that Emma had been asking about him, and when she found out what was happening, had started a search. This was just preliminary information, she informed Evan.

His socked feet quiet on the hardwood floor, Tag headed for what had been the office. He laid the envelope down on the antique desk, his hand rubbing across the wood. He was thankful that nothing had been damaged when it was moved out. A frown covered his face as he pondered just why before he shook his head. Heading for the French doors that opened onto the back porch, he stepped through, looking for Ayron.

Ayron had found her hiding place just as everyone had left. A wicker swing in the corner of the porch had always drawn her. Her parents had let her be if she was there, finally reaching out to her when they felt she had had enough quiet. She looked up as the swing moved and Tag sat beside her.

Reaching for her hand, Tag absentmindedly rubbed his thumb along it. He bit at his lip, not quite sure how to talk with her, not any more. Today had changed something. Coming to her home? That had moved their relationship to somewhere he wasn't sure that they were ready to go. Only God knew what the plan and purpose were of what they were facing. And that was far from over, he knew.

"Okay, my love?" He tilted his head to watch her face.

Ayron finally nodded, wiping at the tears that she could not control.

"I am, I think. This has just been such an upheaval."

Tag sighed. "Evan left me some more material, as did Brownie. Eric is sending up more."

"Can we leave it? I just can't do that tonight." Ayron fought to control her tears. "I just don't get it, Tag. I don't understand why someone would do this to us."

"I don't know. Eric said Ella was still working on the investigation, but not officially. Anything that she finds will be verified by another detective."

"That's good. I like her." Ayron's head went down against Tag's shoulder as she yawned. "We need to pack up at the B&B. We can stay here."

"Already done. Flannery and I went over there earlier. She also insisted on shopping for groceries and other stuff, as she called it, for us. She and Eunice did that while we were sorting out everything here."

"She did? She is such a sweet, giving person." Ayron was silent for a while. "Brownie talked to me, I guess when you and Flannery were away. He had spoken with the coroner. Dad's heart just gave out. I think he died of a broken heart."

"I'm sure that he did." Tag didn't continue but he muttered to himself that he could fully understand that sentiment.

"Where do we go from here, Tag?"

"I'm not sure what you're asking."

"I mean, your work is down south. I have work here. My home is here. Yours is in the south."

"That's a decision we will make together. I am not going anywhere, my love. I will stay with you. As to my work? I am not sure that I will go back."

"You're not?" Ayron was surprised at that and it showed on her face. She studied him, seeing the tiredness and pain that was on his face. "You're afraid to."

Tag nodded. Ayron had understood him enough to realize that.

"I am. I am jumping at noises that I normally wouldn't do. I am looking over my shoulder for someone coming at me. I worry about you." He sighed. "I need to find someone to talk to, who can give me counsel."

"Dad had come across a lady named Darcy at one point. She is a retired forensics psychologist. She told him that if he ever had a friend who needed to talk about things, to call her. In fact, her husband is an officer."

"He is? That's interesting. Yeah, if I need to, I will." Tag studied their hands. "Are you okay with this, what they've done?"

"I am. I wanted to repaint but just didn't have the heart. It's a big undertaking."

"That is it." Tag was silent for a while, praying for her. "What about your work?"

Ayron sighed. "And there's that. I had put in my resignation, actually, wanting to go back to school. I just wasn't sure what I wanted to take."

"You had. Okay, we can figure that out."

Ayron finally rose, heading for the house, a glance at the clock letting her know that it was close to dinner time. She sighed. She had no idea of what Tag liked to eat, but she didn't want a lot. She stood, staring into the open refrigerator, amazed at the selection of food that Flannery had chosen. And she just knew that Flannery would not want to be paid back.

Chapter 15

Landing harshly on his hands and knees the next day, Tag shook his head, not having heard the men who had entered the garage behind him. He just prayed that Ayron would be safe. It didn't appear as if he would be.

"Where is it?" The hard, coarse voice hammered at his ears, even as he tried to orient himself again.

Hauled to his feet and shoved against the door, Tag stared at the men through blurry eyes. *This has to stop, Lord, he thought. I can't do this. Not and keep Ayron safe.* The men walked away a short time later, leaving Tag a crumpled heap near the door. He waited for them to return and didn't hear them.

Shoving himself up to lean against the door, Tag drew in deep breaths, trying to regain his strength. He heard a noise and jumped, his eyes huge with fear as footsteps approached. Eric appeared, a dismayed cry coming from him as he rapidly crossed the garage and was crouched down beside Tag.

"Tag? What happened?"

"I was ambushed again." Tag's face drew taut with his pain. "I can't let Ayron see me like this."

"It's too late for that." Eric looked around as Ayron appeared.

"Tag?" Ayron's shocked cry sounded through the garage as she was beside him almost without moving, her hands reaching for his face. "Them again?"

"I think so. I don't remember them from before. I never got a good look at them." He reached for Eric's hand. "Help me up."

"And to the hospital." Ayron tapped her foot as Tag shook his head. "Yes, you are. We need this documented, don't we, Eric? At least, that's what I think we do."

"You are correct, Ayron. Brownie was on his way here. He can take Tag's statement of facts." Eric shook his head at Ayron, his eyes back on Tag.

Tag finally nodded, agreeing that he would sit in the chair that Ayron pointed to. He was slightly amused at how she was fussing over him but careful not to let her see. Eric just shook his head, turning to walk around the garage both inside and outside. He stood staring at the back gate, turning his head as he heard Brownie approach him.

"Again?"

Eric nodded. "Again. I walked in just after it happened." He sighed. "Now what?"

"I need to talk to both of them about what we have found. And I gather that you have information you need to go over with them."

"I do. Evan said a friend of his has sent material as well. I am not sure that Tag has looked at it." Eric turned to stare behind him at the garage, watching as the paramedics approached it.

———

76

"I would gather not likely. Yesterday was traumatic enough for the two. He's highly worried about Ayron."

"And rightly so." Eric turned to head for the house. "That gate back there? Does Ayron lock it?"

"I have no idea. I would suspect not as it leads to a nature path. And her father had mentioned one time I was speaking with him a year or so ago that she liked to walk it." Brownie turned to stare at the fence. "We'll need to put a lock on it for her. She can't be out walking there right now."

"And that will go hard. Tag said that she had quit her job."

"She had?" Brownie frowned. "She worked for an accountant as his clerk. Somehow that doesn't surprise me that she has. She'll be looking at something else to do."

"And will Tag come back?" Brownie squinted at the sky, one eye closing as he did so. He had thoughts as to what Tag would do but just couldn't express them.

Eric paused, Brownie asking the very question that he had been asking himself.

"You know, I don't rightly know that. Somehow, I suspect not. He's jumping at the smallest sound. We can't have that."

"No, we can't. I have some names I can pass on to him."

"Good. We need to ensure that he gets the help he needs. Ayron as well." Eric turned as Ayron approached. "Ayron?"

"He is refusing to go to the hospital, Eric. Can we please make him?" Tears that she refused to shed hovered in her eyes.

Eric swung an arm around Ayron and turned her back towards where Tag now stood, watching her.

"He's an adult, alert and orientated, as they say. No matter our feelings and wishes, he can refuse. I gather that he has?" Eric watched, a smile lurking in his eyes at the disgruntled nod that Ayron gave.

"He did. He won't leave me. At some point, he has to." Ayron folded her arms across her abdomen as she stood, eyes locked with Tag. "At some point, he will return to work and I will be on my own." A strangled sob came from her as she broke free from Eric's arm and ran for the house, the door closing quietly behind her.

Tag watched her and then approached his two friends.

"Eric? You're here. And so is Brownie. Brownie, you told me that you were off today."

"I am here for a friend. I know right well that you didn't go over any of that material yesterday. You need our input." Brownie smirked at Tag as Tag just shook his head. "Now, can we find your lady and proceed with that very task?"

Eric grinned at Tag as well.

"I have to head back last this afternoon. I took a couple of days of personal leave but I have an appointment tomorrow afternoon that I need to be at. Let's see what we can discover from the mass of material that we have."

Tag walked towards the house, his steps slowing as he approached Ayron, finally stopping just in front of her. He ducked his head, seeing the devastation and worry and yes, terror, that she was trying hard to hide.

"Ayron? What is it?"

Ayron just shook her head. "It's everything, Tag. Just everything. That Emma, whoever she is, has sent more stuff by courier. Who is she, anyway?"

Chapter 16

Wrapping Ayron into a tight hug, Tag prayed for her, audible only to the two of them. He felt Ayron relax slightly against him.

"Emma? She's a friend of ours. She finds information that no one else can find. And her husband has a security team."

"Security team? As in?" She leaned back to look up at him, her eyes narrowing at his look.

"Security team. As in training other teams. As in they will provide protection when asked as that is what they used to do."

"And do you think that we will need that?"

Tag shrugged, his eyes on Brownie. "We may. We'll talk about it. No decision that way will be made without your input or mine, unless it becomes a matter of life and death."

Ayron searched his face with her eyes, a frown in place, before she nodded.

"I get that, Tag. I just don't know if we will be able to." She hugged him, the first that she had made an effort to do that on her own. "I hate this. You need to go on with your life and you can't. Not while you're married to me and not while we are going through this."

Tag spoke without thinking, his eyes on the top of her head.

"Maybe I don't want to move on. Maybe I want to stay, right here, with you. Maybe that's what God's plan is."

Ayron froze at his words, not moving, wonder in her mind. *God, is this You? Is this Your plan? For us to be married? But I don't get it. I really just don't. I know You promise protection and safety but not necessarily that we won't go through stuff. I hate this for Tag's sake, though, dear Lord. Please protect him.*

The couple finally moved back towards the house, finding Brownie and Eric awaiting them. Tag reached for the coffee that Brownie had poured for him, finding his place at the table, just staring at the material piled there.

"Where do we start?" Tag reached for it at last, leafing through it.

"That's a good question." Eric looked through the pile that he had picked up. "There's a lot here. And none of us are investigators."

Ayron stood, her back to the kitchen counter, watching the men before she set aside her own mug, reached for all the material to the men's surprise and headed for the home office. Eric was on his feet, following her.

"Ayron? What are you up to?"

"I need to make copies of all this for each of you and the detective who is investigating it. Then, we collate it as to date, place, time, people. That makes sense to do that, doesn't it?" Ayron looked up at him.

"It does. Here, let me help."

The pair worked away, copying and sorting the material. Ayron stared at it for a moment, not quite sure what they all had. Eric watched her closely, seeing just how close to collapsing she was. He finally reached for all the material, a grin on his face as she protested.

"It's okay, Ayron. Here. I'll take it. Do we work in here or the kitchen?"

"It doesn't really matter." She frowned. "I don't see that Dad's computer or my laptop came back. Did they take them?"

Tag hesitated in the doorway as he heard her words and then shared a look with Brownie.

"I don't see that we reported that, Ayron. Did we, Brownie?"

Brownie shook his head. "No, I don't think we did." His phone was out as he called it in. "Anything else that you see missing?"

Ayron stared around. "No. Unless." She was across the room, reaching for one of the bookcases and swinging it open. The men stared at her and then it, and Tag was behind as she entered.

"What is this, Ayron?"

"A secret room." She grinned up at him for a moment. "Dad found it one day by accident. We didn't know it was here. Let me see if for some reason the computer is in here." Her hand reached for a switch and light flooded the room. She stared around and then pointed. "There. There they are. Now, how?"

"Did anyone know about this?"

She stared at Eric as he asked the question. "Just our neighbour next door. He was really good friends with Mom and Dad. I wonder."

Brownie was away and out of the room, intent on finding the neighbour. He was back in short order.

"Your neighbour put them in here. He snuck in, he said, as the men were packing up the house. He has been able to provide a good description to the investigating officer. He was trying to reach you to let you know but your phone just went to voice mail."

"I know it did. I have no idea where it is." She stared at Tag as he held up a phone. "That's mine. Now, did he put it in here as well?"

"He may have without knowing that it was yours. Can you open it?" He watched as she tried. "Does it need charging?"

"It does." Ayron was away from them, heading for the desk, searching it. She stopped, a puzzled look on her face.

"Ayron?" Brownie stood beside her, his phone still in his head.

"The desk has been cleared out. Where is everything? I mean, there were no documents in it. That was all locked away, in that room." Ayron stabbed a finger towards the open room. "But there were other things. My phone charger for one."

Tag wrapped his arms around her from behind. "We'll figure it out, but it is a puzzle. Did the lawyer ever get found?"

Brownie was staring at his phone, reading the text message that he had just received before he looked up and shared a look with both Tag and Eric.

"He was, but he's refusing to talk. He has been arrested. And we have more trouble. The people who said they had bought the house? They've lodged a trespassing and theft complaint against Ayron."

Chapter 17

Frowning, Brownie paced through the house before heading for the garage. He searched for boxes, not finding any. Scanning the area, he suddenly turned and reached for a ladder, setting it against the end of the house that the attached garage was against. He could faintly see the outline of a door.

Eric stood and watched, having following him out.

"Brownie?"

"There's an opening here, Eric. Ask Ayron where it leads to."

"It leads to the attic, Brownie. That's the only way in." Ayron stood at the foot of the ladder, her head tilting back as she watched him intently. "Why do you need to know?"

"Because I don't think that we knew it was here. I don't remember hearing anyone speak of searching it." He felt around the edge, trying to open the door.

"Upper right corner of the door. Push hard against it. It has a magnetic catch. Dad didn't want anyone to know it was there." Ayron bit at her lips as she remembered her father's words.

Brownie shot her a look and then pressed where she had told him to, surprised that the door popped open. He moved slightly to open it all the way and then looked around.

"Do you have a flashlight, Ayron?"

Ayron shook her head. "You won't need one. There is a light switch on the left inside the door."

Brownie stared in amazement as the light flooded the room.

"Ayron? Were there a lot of boxes up here?"

"No, I had emptied it. There should be nothing there. There is?" Ayron was puzzled.

"There are a number. I suggest we bring them all down and then sort them out to see what we have. There are like twenty or more."

The men moved to do just that, Ayron standing staring at the boxes, a frown on her face, before she moved to search the outside of them.

"That's not my writing." She looked up as Tag swung an arm around her. "Who did this?"

"We'll work through them. Eric does have to leave, but Brownie can stay. Evan and Flannery will be here shortly." Tag pulled out his phone. "And Micah and Luke are on their way."

"And just who are Micah and Luke?"

"They work for Abe. You know? That security team we're trying to avoid?" Tag grinned at her, mischief lurking in his eyes.

"Oh, them." She tilted her hand to read the text. "And who is Ian?"

"Ian? Another one of Abe's men." Tag looked up, sharing a look with Eric. "He's who we need. He's a paralegal. He can help."

They all turned as they heard a sound outside, Eric and Brownie moving that way, leaving Tag standing with Ayron.

"Can we help you?" Brownie's voice sounded loud in the sudden stillness.

The two men, in work clothes, looked up from where they had been unloading lumber.

"Not really. The new homeowners have hired us to put up a shed in the backyard. So, if you'll excuse us?"

"Not so fast." Brownie saw the couple approaching and then two patrol officers walking their way. "This house is not for sale and has not been sold. The owner is in the garage and I know for a fact that she has not hired any workmen.

The older man sneered at him. "We have a signed contract. So I suggest you move or we'll call the police."

Brownie sighed, reaching for his identification and holding it up.

"How convenient that you want to do that. I am the police. And there are two patrol officers right behind you."

The men paled, their hands holding the lumber stilling as they stared first at Brownie and then the officers standing behind them. The couple had approached, the man sneering at the officers.

—

"Go ahead with your work. Officers, arrest these people for trespassing." The man glared at them when they refused to move. "Arrest them, or we will have your badges."

Brownie shook his head, a frown hovering over his face for a moment as he watched the three men walking towards him. Law enforcement, he thought. They have that look.

Tag appeared beside him, his eyes watchful, nodding at the three. Brownie caught the look on his face and then nodded at well.

"Your friends?"

"They are." Tag watched as Micah moved past him towards the garage door where Ayron was hovering.

Micah's face was grim as he approached her.

"You're Ayron?" At her nod, he smiled. "I'm Micah. Abe said he would let Tag know we were on our way."

"He did. Thank you. Now what? They don't own this place. I never signed anything to change ownership. We think the lawyer dummied it all up. And Brownie got word that they want me charged for trespassing and theft."

Micah stood beside her, his eyes on the confrontation in front of them.

"Abe had heard that. Emma is digging up information on these two and also your lawyer and funnelling to the police here and to you and to the investigating officer in Tag's town. We'll sort it out.

Right now, we'll have them removed and then work with you to keep you safe."

"We can do that?" Ayron shivered, feeling fear building up inside her. "It's not over, Micah."

"No, it's not. Kataleen, my wife, and I went through some really hard stuff in our adventure as we term it. So did all the guys on our team, including Abe and Emma." He wasn't watching her, his focus intent of assessing the area to be prepared to move her to safety.

"You did? Do I need to talk to them?"

Micah grinned. "Yeah, it wouldn't hurt. And we have other friends who have had the same. They would gladly talk to you."

Chapter 18

Tag walked back towards Ayron, Eric beside him, before he turned, a thought crossing his mind. He shook his head, turning once more to study the boxes that they had pulled down. Micah's gaze shifted between Tag and Ayron and then raised as Luke walked his way. Micah moved away to speak with Luke, both men turning to watch the growing commotion on the driveway.

"They just aren't giving up, are they?" Luke kept his voice low. "Abe would want to move Ayron and Tag away from here."

"And she won't go. She's digging in to fight. She doesn't have to say anything. We know only too well what it's like."

"That we do." Luke winced as Brownie took a blow to the face, that knocked him backwards, Eric just catching him from falling flat. "That won't go over well. Nope, there you go!"

"And he knew Brownie is an officer?" Micah turned as he heard a sound behind him. "Ayron?"

"I know him. I didn't recognize him. But he's been around town since just before Dad went. And I think he was with the lawyer?" She looked up horrified. "What did I do?"

"You did nothing." Eric spoke from beside her. "They did. He'll be charged. I have an investigator

---

90

heading this way." He frowned as he glanced at his watch. "Listen, you two. I have to run. Tag? Let me know when you're heading back down. I'll have someone come and get you two."

Ayron turned away, tired of the commotion, tired of feeling as if she had no life, tired of being chased and hounded and unsafe. Tag watched her, seeing her heading for the boxes, and followed her.

"Ayron?"

"Tag? Who did this? And what is in them? How do we know that what was taken from my house is even in them?" Ayron stood, her arms wrapped around her abdomen, staring at the far garage wall, her thoughts muddled.

Tag paused, knowing that she was correct. He turned to look for Brownie, seeing him approaching with someone who had to be a detective, Tag thought.

Brownie paused for a moment, a hand rubbing at his face. He really hadn't seen that coming but he should have, he knew. Now what, he wondered? Titus was there, as a friend but also as a detective. Brownie introduced him and then stepped back, his eyes still on the vehicles parked out front. He could hear the woman's raised voice, just not make out her words. This was not how today was to have gone, he thought. He turned as he heard Ayron's voice raised in surprise and then worry.

Ian held up a hand, not surprised at Ayron's response. She didn't know him, after all, and what he had said would have been a surprise to her.

"Ian? What's going on?" Tag wrapped his arms around Ayron, finding her stance tense but fearful.

—

"I just asked if she had a lawyer. And if she didn't, then she should have."

"Ian's right, my love. You do need a lawyer. Just to protect you and your property. Something is off here."

"I know. I know he's right. I just don't know who to trust here in town." Ayron blinked rapidly, not wanting the tears clouding her eyes to fall. She hated to cry and especially in front of anyone.

"Ayron, I know of a lawyer in a nearby town. He was a friend of Abe's father. If you wish, I can call him and he would meet with you."

"He can't do that!" Ayron was horrified at the thought.

"He can and he will." Ian turned as he heard footsteps. "And here is he. Did Abe call you, Ted?"

"He did. Just asked if I would stop by. He didn't have any details, other than Evan was concerned about you. It looks as if Evan was right." Ted Fletcher was dressed casually in jeans and a sweatshirt. He grinned at Ayron. "You must be the lady in distress, as they said. And just what are we doing with all these boxes?"

"Thank you. I am. And I have no idea what we are doing with them. Brownie pulled them out of the attic. That attic should have been empty." Ayron turned to study the boxes. "And before you ask, there are no other secret rooms. Just that one off the office. And the attic that is sort of hidden."

Two hours later, the men stood back, their eyes shifting between Ayron and the boxes. They had searched them all, finding Ayron's missing belongings, but also items that she was adamant were not hers. Brownie had left and then returned, a crime scene tech in tow, who began to document the items that Ayron insisted were not hers.

Tag moved Ayron from the garage into the house, nodding as Ian, Luke and Micah headed for their vehicle. They would be back, he knew. He was grateful that Abe had reached out to Ted. His gentle teasing and quiet comments had helped to calm Ayron, and that had been needed, badly. The others had shot her looks over the hours and then watched him. Tag knew that they had questions, questions to which he had no answer.

Ayron paced away from Tag, heading for the office, finding her phone and plugging it in. She just knew there would be multiple messages that she didn't want to deal with. Her hand paused as she set her phone down, her eyes on the vase of peach-coloured roses that sat on the desk. Suddenly afraid, she hesitated to reach for the envelope that contained the card.

This is silly, she thought. With all those guys around, nothing should have happened. Her fingers opened the flap and she slid out the card, her other hand covering her mouth in surprise.

Tag stood where he could watch her, a smile on his face as he saw her reaction to the flowers. *I shouldn't have surprised her, he thought, but I just had to.*

Ayron read the card, her fingers over her mouth to still her words. Tag had done this. Somehow or

---

93

other over the day, he had arranged for flowers to be delivered to her. Her thumb ran over the words. She stilled, wondering if he really did mean them.

"So glad you are the part of my heart I didn't know I was missing. All my love. Tag."

Chapter 19

Early the next morning, early enough that the sun was barely peeking over the horizon, Tag stood in the kitchen, watching the coffee slowly drip into the coffee pot. He had not slept well. The headaches that he thought were diminishing had returned, and that pain had kept him from his sleep. He yawned, rubbing at his eyes, his thoughts reverting to the previous day.

Tag was puzzled. He had no idea who that couple was and why they kept insisting that they had bought the house. He knew that Brownie would be working with the investigator on that. And Ted had promised to look into it. When he heard the name of the lawyer, Art Archer, his face had closed but he had simply nodded. Tag figured that he knew something about the man that wasn't good. Ian had indicated to him that Emma was finding more information than what they had thought was available, as she always did.

Ayron stood for a moment watching Tag, seeing the pain in his drawn face. She had heard him up and down and moving around overnight. Her prayer had been for him, for herself, for whatever it was that they were facing. And just what that was, she really wasn't sure.

Turning as he heard her footsteps, Tag watched Ayron as she approached him, moving into his space and into his hug. He held her, swaying slightly from fatigue, before she turned him and forced him to sit.

"You need help, Tag. Let me call someone. Or at least take you somewhere to be seen." Ayron was that concerned.

Tag gave a brief nod, to do more was impossible, he thought. The headache was intense, but he refused to give into it. He watched Ayron through blurry eyes, not hearing a tap at the door, and was surprised when she moved away.

Thurlow stood and observed his son, shaking his head. Tag was in pain, he knew, and would just refuse to give into it. His eyes lifted to Ayron as she worked at the counter, turning to find Tag standing right behind her. His amusement grew as he saw her frustration at Tag before she made him sit again, turning to retrieve the cup of coffee that she had poured for him.

Tag sensed someone else in the room and turned rapidly in his chair, his hand coming up to the side of his head as the headache pounded.

"Dad?"

"Yes, son. I'm here. Now, about that head? What have you taken?" Thurlow just shook his head at Ayron, who stood with her hands gripping the back of a chair. He dropped the file folders that he had been holding onto the table and then reached to pour his own mug of coffee, turning to find Ayron had sat beside Tag, her hand on his. He once more shook his head, knowing that the two young people in front of him were dancing around one another and their growing feelings for each other.

———

"I can't, Dad. You know any pain medications knock me out and make me sleep. I need to stay awake. Ayron needs me to do that." Tag's head dropped as he spoke, his eyes squeezed tight against the pain.

"You're not doing her any good as you are." Thurlow simply reached to pull his son to his feet. "Off to bed again, son. Ayron, do you have an ice pack? We can place it on his neck, at the base of the skull. That will help."

"I do. Or a hot water bottle." She walked ahead of him to the bathroom to fill the hot water bottle, turning with both the ice pack and hot water bottle in her hands.

"We'll try the ice pack first. Then the hot water bottle." Thurlow saw the worry deep in her eyes. Once he had his son settled, he moved back to her, drawing her into a hug and then arm around her shoulders, back down the stairs to the kitchen. "He was awake early. I doubt that he slept much. Now, sit, my dear. Let me fix you something."

"Just coffee for now. Thank you, Mr. Rafferty." She looked up as she heard his steps pause.

"It's Thurlow, my dear, or Dad. Whichever you prefer. You're one of our family now. A treasured part."

Ayron stared at him for a moment, then looked away, still not sure about that very fact. She pointed to the file folders.

"What have you found out?"

Thurlow grinned at her, looking like his son for a moment.

"I like you. Direct and to the point." He sobered. "First, can I pray with you? Then I'll go over what I have."

"You have had to be on the road early today, Thurlow."

"I pulled in really late last night and took a motel room. I'll stay for a couple of days." He held up a hand as her mouth opened. "No, I stay there, Ayron."

Ayron finally agreed, a disgruntled look briefly flitting across her face. She really was not sure of anything anymore, that much she knew. Thurlow was stepping in to take care of her, just as her father would have. She willed the welling tears back down, not wanting them to be obvious. Ayron didn't see the look of compassion that Thurlow sent her way before he reached for the first file folder.

"Ayron, the lawyer that your father had? He has been disbarred and has been for at least six months."

"He has? How did we not know that?" Ayron sat back, a hand rubbing up and down her arm. "That was around when Dad went. He handled the estate or part of it. There was a lot that I had to do. He just didn't answer my calls. Is that why?"

"More than likely. He could not have sold your home, not for him to pretend to act in a legal manner. You understand that?" He smiled at her vigorous nod. "Now, as to that couple? We have traced them to being a relative of his. The man has been charged with assaulting a police officer, trespass, attempted fraud, for starters. Did you know that your home could never be sold until you reach a certain age?"

"That's what Mom and Dad said. I had forgotten. I can't until I am thirty and I'm not that yet." Ayron sat back, relief in her bearing. "So, where do we go from here? How do we find out why?"

"There's a lot of information here that you need to go over. I understand that Abe found a lawyer for you. Trust him. He's good. He'll look after you. And he will not charge you."

"But, he has to!" Ayron was horrified and then upset at the thought.

"No, Ayron. He has already said that he won't. He never charges friends. And that is what you are. With you married to Tag, that makes you friends with him. He will take care of it all for you. He called me yesterday, asking me to investigate the lawyer and the so-called new owner of your home that is not the owner."

Ayron spluttered and then sank back, relief in her heart.

"Is this what God does, Thurlow? Is this how He takes care of us? By bringing people into our lives?"

"He does, child. That He does. He brought you and Tag together, and the reason for that we are still working on. I understand that there were a number of items found in your attic that don't belong to you. It is an active investigation, and the investigator here and at home will keep you updated on their findings as much as they can. Ted will too." He reached to refill their coffee cups. "Now, what can we do for you?"

—

Chapter 20

Rolling over to this side, Tag groaned. His headache had eased but it was still there enough that he felt disabled. This is not how he wanted to feel. He needed to be up and around, to protect his lady love. Tag finally acknowledged to himself that he loved Ayron deeply. He could see her opening up to him, her sense of humour peeking through every once in a while. Reaching for his phone, Tag scrolled through his text messages. Good, he thought. Evan and Flannery were heading their way, bringing a meal for them.

Showered, shaved, and feeling somewhat more human, Tag slowly walked down the stairs, stopping at the bottom as he heard voices. Dad's here, he thought. When did he arrive? And that sounds like Brownie as well. But there is someone else.

Tag jumped as he felt a hand touch his back and then heard an indrawn breath. Ayron had approached him, not knowing that he hadn't heard her.

"Ayron? Where did you come from?" Tag reached to hug her, holding on longer than he normally would have, sensing that she needed that contact with him.

"From behind you. You didn't hear me." She peered up at him. "How is the head? And don't tell me that the headache is gone."

"It's still there." He looked towards the office. "Dad's here?"

"He is. He pulled in really early this morning. Like just as the sun was coming up. Like at the same time that you were trying your best to stay on your feet in the kitchen and watch the coffee drip." Ayron could not resist teasing him, her eyes sparkling with mischief even as she watched him closely.

"I don't remember him coming at all. I don't even remember getting up. The headache was that bad." He sighed. "I have to decide what to do, you know. I don't know if I can continue as an officer, not with the headaches. And I am jumping at every little sound. And I can't handle someone coming up and surprising me. Not yet anyway." Tag watched the emotions flickering across her face. "Not you, my love. Not you. I can tell when you are around me."

"Really? You could have fooled me. I thought I would have to scrape you off the ceiling just now." Ayron smirked at him. "Listen, Brownie is here. Evan and Flannery are on their way, stating that they are bringing dinner. And somebodies named Eunice and Everett have shown up, told me that they knew you, and then just moved in to research with your father. Everett told me he wants to take a look at your head. Any idea why?"

Tag turned her towards the kitchen, smelling the aroma of freshly brewed coffee.

"I do. He's a retired paramedic and wants to make sure I am okay. Eunice used to work in a large city police department and is part of the local force in her town. Did Dooley come?"

"Dooley? That's a different name." She pretended to think about it and then shook her head. "Nope, no one by that name. Not yet. And your Dad has provided a lot of information, including that Art Archer was disbarred around the time Dad died."

"He was? That's interesting." Tag reached for the mug of coffee Eunice handed him. "Thanks, Eunice. And just what have you discovered?"

Eunice shook her head, even as a smile crossed her face. "Later, Tag. Right now, Everett is waiting for you. Let him take a look at you. Your wife is very concerned. Apparently, you were not making a lot of sense this morning."

"No? I don't even remember being up this morning." He squinted at the clock. "I don't think I had a lot of sleep last night. I crashed."

"And you will. You need to rest, Tag." Everett spoke from behind him. "You took a beating that almost killed you. That will take time for you to recover from physically." Both Tag and Everett understood what Everett had not said, that he needed to recover in other ways.

Tag submitted to Everett's exam, knowing that if the older man felt it necessary, he would simply pack him up and take him in to the hospital. Everett watched him closely, seeing how close to the edge of collapse he was and sighed. *Tag,* he thought, *you just can't do this. You need to sleep and I know you're not going to, not while Ayron is in trouble. And just what trouble that is? We're starting to get a picture and it's not pretty. Not that it ever is.*

Ayron had watched closely, her eyes narrowed at the pain that Tag was trying too hard to hide. She sighed and then moved to sit beside him, her hand reaching for his, feeling the roughness of his against the softness of hers.

"Tag? Please? You need to rest. If you need to take your pain medications so that you sleep, then that's what you do. You can't continue like this. We need you to." She paused, biting at her lower lip, her eyes raised to the ceiling. "God help me, Tag. I need you to. You're the only one who can help me make sense of this." She looked at him, finding his eyes locked on her face. "You were there. Even though you don't remember a lot, you were there. You tried to help me before we were abducted. And then you tried so hard to prevent us from being married."

"I know, my love. I know. It's just that I feel everything caving in on us and I want to prevent that."

"I know, but you can't. Your dad has found some interesting items. Emma has called him, I think. Ted is here as well, working through what we have, just from a legal standpoint. Your father mentioned Dad's will, that I can never sell the house. I had forgotten. So how did that lawyer think he could?" She was on her feet, heading for the door as she heard a knock, leaving the three in the kitchen staring after her.

"Did she really just do that?" Tag moved to rise, worried that an enemy had appeared and would make Ayron disappear.

"Your father's there. I hear Dooley. So, she's safe. But we do need to speak with her, Tag." Eunice's hand rested on his head for a moment. "Let me. It may be better if it comes from an authority figure."

"And that would be you." Flannery reached to hug Eunice, before she stared at Tag. "You look horrible, Tag."

"Thanks, Flannery. You know how to make a person feel so good." Tag grinned at her, even as he stood and wrapped an arm around Ayron. "Where are we working?"

"In the office, but we eat first." Thurlow had appeared, Evan with him. "We have food. Let's eat, people, pray, and then see where we stand."

Chapter 21

Late that night, Tag studied his notes. He was not an investigator but he had developed instincts as a patrol officer that he was trying hard to use right then. Everyone had left and he had heard Ayron moving around upstairs. He sighed. He would soon need to retire, but he didn't want to. Dreams or nightmares or whatever you wanted to call them had begun to haunt him. Tag knew that he could not have done anything different with Ayron, but he was still puzzled as to why. The information that they were all digging up wasn't helping. If anything, Tag thought, it was confusing them.

Ayron moved to sit beside him, her eyes on the floor. Tag watched her face before he began to pray for her.

"Tag? What do we do? How do we stay safe? And once again, where is God in all this?"

"He's here, my love. Right here. There are times when we feel the darkness closing in, that we don't feel His presence, that we feel abandoned." Ayron's eyes were on him. "That's when He's there. He is sheltering us in the rock, covering us with His hand, protecting us. We may never know exactly why we go through what we do. But I know He's here. He's been here all along. He has protected you, in ways you probably don't even know. He loves you that much, Ayron, more than I do." Tag had not realized that he had made that declaration, but Ayron stared at him.

"Tag? What did you just say?" Ayron waited. "Tag?"

Tag groaned. "I said that I loved you. You're not ready to hear that."

"And says who? You? The world?" Ayron blinked back tears. "Do you know how I have longed and prayed for someone to tell me that?" She was on her feet, running from the room, Tag staring after her before he followed her, to find her standing on the back deck, the light from the moon and the stars the only illumination.

"I didn't think you were ready, Ayron. And you should have had a say in it, to go on dates, be given flowers and chocolates or whatever it is you like, to be wooed or courted or whatever word you would want to use. And you weren't.'"

Ayron was shaking her head. "It doesn't matter, Tag. Not the visible physical things. What matters is the person's heart. You have shown me yours. We need to get through whatever this is and then talk."

Tag turned suddenly, pulling Ayron with him towards the door, hoping to make it inside. Only, he didn't get a chance. He was on the floor, his hands bound behind him before he could make much of a move. Ayron's scream was cut off by a hand across her mouth before she was lifted bodily and carried away, through the gate at the back of the yard, and to a waiting vehicle. She was shoved roughly inside, forced to the floor and her own hands bound. Tag landed beside her, a groan coming from him as he hit hard.

Ayron's heart raced, not sure exactly what had happened, other than they were captive once again. And who had them this time? Thurlow and Brownie had agreed. There was more than one group involved, competing it seemed. But just what they were after? Neither man could say. The investigator had been around, Ben Richard, just to talk with her earlier, when Tag had still been asleep. His keen eyes had watched her, but he couldn't give her much more information than what she had been given.

Tag lay still, his head pounding, a groan that he could not control torn from him. They were captive again, he thought. Who and why? That wasn't clear. Not at all. He felt the vehicle moving forward, gathering speed and then turning abruptly. The drive had not been that long, but where had they ended up? That he didn't know and if he didn't know, then how could he protect his lady?

Art Archer watched as the camper the two were in pulled into the old barn. He had found this place, abandoned and run down, and just taken it over. The owner had not wanted to sign the paperwork, but Art had had his way. The owner was no longer around, and Art had no regrets. That old man had stood in his way and paid the ultimate price. It was not the first time that had happened. He watched from the shadows as Ayron and Tag were pulled from the camper and then forced up the ladder to the haymow, to where the cell was waiting. He had planned this for months, Ayron his target. Only someone else had stepped in and forced the pair to marry. She was to marry him, that had been his plan, even though he was old enough to be her father. He had plans for her, plans that did not include Tag.

Thurlow stood on the back deck the next morning, searching the yard for his son and his wife, not seeing them. He strode across the porch, his hand reaching for the knob, finding it turning under his hand. Sudden fear for the pair had him stepping backwards, away from the house, pulling out his phone and calling for help.

Brownie approached him, the crime scene techs searching the house and outside, before one of them headed for the back gate. Thurlow watched from the side of the yard, fear in his heart for them, knowing from the look on Brownie's face that they were not in there.

"Brownie?"

"Thurlow, they're not in the house. It looks as if they haven't been since last night. Their supper dishes are still on the table, the coffee pot hasn't been emptied, and I know Tag does that at night and sets it for the next morning. They have just disappeared."

"Where's that lawyer?" Thurlow felt anger towards the man building in him and prayed to have it removed, as difficult as that seemed to be.

"He made his bail and disappeared. We're looking for him. Other forces have been in touch, now that we have reached out. He's a nasty bit of work."

"And I suspect that he has murdered people?"

"That's what we are hearing." Brownie excused himself and moved towards the tech near the gate, their conversation brief before Brownie headed back to the house. "They were taken out the gate, Thurlow, to a vehicle. We're not sure what kind yet, but the techs will do their best to determine it."

"And where would they be taken?" Thurlow's mind was racing. He pulled out his phone as he felt it vibrating and sighed. Meg had sent him a text, worried about Tag. She had that sense of when her sons were in difficulty or needed help. He paused and then excused himself to walk away. Meg needed to know, and once she did, nothing would keep her away.

Chapter 22

Three days had gone by, three long days with searches made throughout Ayron's hometown and into the surrounding area. Nothing had been found. No one had seen them. Thurlow had not slept, unable to do so for worry about his son. Meg had grown white and quiet, her task making sure that the men and women who were searching were taken care of. Tully and his wife and son had appeared, Tully taking up the searches on the computer, racing to find what information he could. Emma had continued to forward material to them, sending Abe at one point to talk with Thurlow and Brownie.

Then, a source on the street had appeared at Brownie's home, staying in the dark shadows late that third night, warning Brownie that the couple's lives were at stake but he had an idea of where they were. Did Brownie want to know? Brownie had taken one look at the youth and then pulled him into the house, the lights dim, and sat the youth down. He did want to know and just how did that information come to him? The youth, Danny by name, simply shrugged. He got around town, living on the streets, and had heard rumours of a lawyer that had turned bad.

Brownie had taken the information and then headed for the station, determined to prove that the lawyer had them and making sure that they had the warrants that they needed. He didn't want anything to fall through the cracks, he thought.

———

Early the next morning, early enough that it was still dark, Brownie and some of his fellow officers quietly approached the property, seeing no vehicles and only a dim light in the house. They separated, some heading for the house, Brownie and three other officers heading for the barn.

They crept in quietly, their flashlights showing the old farm machinery and empty stalls. Brownie headed for the ladder, one of the officers on his heels, and climbed. Both men stopped abruptly as they saw the cell. The flashlights moved across the area and then back, showing the forms of Tag and Ayron as they lay on the floor, motionless. Brownie gave a muted cry and sprang for the door, asking quietly for bolt cutters. The officer was away and back in no time, bolt cutters in hand, reaching to cut through the lock.

The lock gone, the door open, the two hastened forward, dropping to their knees, hands reaching to feel for signs of life. Brownie had Tag up and over his shoulders, heading for the stairs that they had not seen at first, even as the other officer gathered Ayron into his arms and followed.

Rushing them towards the waiting paramedics, Tag could hear a commotion from the house and shot a glance that way. *No,* he thought, *my duty is right here. There are men and women who can deal with that.* His eyes on his friends, he waited, reaching to help and then climbing into the paramedic rig, watching as both Tag and Ayron were placed on stretchers inside. They lay unmoving. He could hear the quiet words of the paramedic as he spoke into his radio and then watched through the door window as they moved away from the property. He frowned. He knew the owner and that owner just would not have been party to this. But then, he had not seen the man for a while. Brownie sighed. There was another avenue of investigation that opened up and he feared for the man's life.

Thurlow and Meg were waiting for Brownie as he approached, grim looks on their faces. Tully had taken a look at them when the call came and simply shaken his head. He would stay at the house, waiting for further word on the investigation. He had searches running. All he asked was that he be called with Tag's condition and with Ayron's as well.

"Brownie?" Meg reached to hug him. "How are they?"

"They were unconscious, Meg, Thurlow. The physicians are with them now. It will be a while." He pointed to some chairs. "Let's sit."

"What can you tell us, Brownie?" Thurlow watched him closely, seeing the anger in the younger man.

"We found them in an abandoned barn. Someone had set up a cell and that's where they were. They are unconscious. I can't tell you why or what their condition is."

"Did you find who took them?" Thurlow had to tamp down his own anger and desire for vengeance. That vengeance was God's to mete out.

Brownie shook his head. "No, but we have an idea of who. That's part of the investigation and I can't divulge it."

———

"We understand. We just want to know that you are after whoever did this." Thurlow was on his feet, following Meg as the physician appeared, looking for them.

"You're Taggart's parents?" His keen eyes studied the older couple.

"We are. Ayron's his wife and should be talking with you. What can you tell us?"

"Was Taggart injured recently?"

"He was. He was beaten severely a couple of weeks ago. He is still fighting severe headaches. Why?" Thurlow's eyes were on his son, standing just outside the door to the room.

"Okay. That explains it. He's coming around but is disoriented as to where and when. He did state that he hadn't had anything to eat or drink in a few days. We're working on rehydrating him."

"Any other injuries?" Meg's hand was in her husband, holding on as tight as she could.

"He has been beaten again, I would suspect to try and protect his wife."

"What about Ayron? He's her only next of kin." Meg was worried about Ayron.

The physician gave Meg a gentle smile. "We know, Mrs. Rafferty. Ayron is well known and loved in our community. I don't know that she is aware of that. We all grieved when her father passed away. It's okay. We can speak with you." He turned for a moment to speak with one of the nurses. "She's the same. Dehydrated. Some new bruising. No other injuries that we can see. She has been rousing now that she's under treatment, but she is distressed and we need to remove that."

"Once she and Tag are together, that will likely help. Can we do that?" Thurlow watched as Tag moved restlessly.

"We can. That is my suggestion, that we get them together. I heard Everett is heading your way. He'll help. Once we have run the IVs and they're more alert, we'll let them go home. He can watch for any signs that they need to come back. I spoke with the police. They want to move them somewhere they can be safe."

"And that would be where? I know Ayron. She will want to go home and not leave there to go anywhere else." Meg walked away with those words, heading for her son. She was on a mission and Thurlow gave a quick grin. No one stood in Meg's way when she was.

Brownie stood beside him. "We'll move them home. I have offers coming in for men and ladies to come and protect them. But neither one of them will agree."

"No, neither one will." Thurlow sighed. "Tag said that he and Ayron had spoken of a security team and when they would ask for that. Tag seemed to think that Ayron would never do that, not willingly."

Brownie shook his head. "No, Ayron won't. That's when you or Tag or one of us will have to make that decision. Abe has volunteered his team and he has other teams that have spoken to him about that."

Chapter 23

Rolling to his side, his headache somewhat eased, Tag felt the softness under his head and the warmth of blankets covering him. He roused somewhat, enough to hear a soft voice but not enough to understand what was being said to him. He sank back down into the darkness that called his name, not willing to come back to reality, to know that Ayron was gone, that the love of his life had been made to disappear. That was what had been threatened. Tag just didn't know how he would live without her. He pleaded with God to protect her, to keep her with him, to heal them both, and then surrendered his wishes to God's plans.

On her knees, her hand holding Tag's, her face wet with her tears, Ayron begged Tag to awaken, to come back to her. Her tears turned to heart-wrenching sobs as her free arm encircled him and her face was buried against his neck, those very tears soaking his T-shirt.

Meg watched, sorrowing at the younger woman's sobs, before she moved to her and drew her to her feet and away. Ayron's face turned back towards Tag, even as she struggled to get free and return to him. Thurlow was there, his arms around his two ladies, drawing both away from the door even as Everett shut it quietly and returned to assess Tag. Everett was worried, worried that Tag had really not roused that much in the two days since they had brought him home.

Ayron paced the house later that morning, devastation in her demeanour. Brownie had been around and Eric had called, a conference call that Brownie had arranged. When informed that it had been Art Archer who had abducted them and held them captive, she had not been surprised. But the shock that she had felt when she was told why still reverberated through her. To think that he had planned to marry her? She shuddered at the thought, just thankful that he had been arrested once more and transported from the area to face further charges elsewhere. Brownie had not told her all that they had found. He simply said that they couldn't. Ayron had taken a look at his face and sighed.

"George is dead, isn't he?" She had refused to back away until Brownie had nodded. "He did that. He was a good friend to our family. Is he getting rid of everyone?"

"He's trying. With the rundown condition of the farm and George not able to maintain it, it appears that Archer just moved in and took over. We have documents that say that."

"But where is George? Buried on the property somewhere? I haven't seen him in months." Ayron paced away in an angry manner before she paused and dropped her head. Lord, I need to give You my anger and fear and I just don't want to. I want to hold on to it and let it burn and simmer. I know that's not right. Please, dear Lord, heal my Tag.

Ayron spun and stomped back towards Brownie, not seeing the smile on Thurlow and Tully's faces as they watched.

"Now what, Brownie? What about that couple?"

"Yes, that couple. They are still in custody. She has been charged with fraud. He has been charged with fraud, trespass, and assault on an officer, just for starters." Brownie shared a look with Thurlow.

"Just who are they?" Ayron spun to stare at Thurlow and Tully when Brownie didn't respond. "Who are they? I need to know."

"You do." Brownie's arm came around her shoulders and he moved her to a chair at the kitchen table before he sat across from her, taking with thanks the mug of coffee handed him. "He is the son of Archer's cousin. They have done this before. Only those people are not around now for us to talk to."

Ayron paled. "He killed them?" Her voice was barely above a whisper. "Did Dad not know?"

"He knew, Ayron." Thurlow pulled out the chair beside her and sat, compassion on his face. "We've been going through your father's papers, and you did tell us we could."

"I remember." Her eyes were glued to his face, not even blinking Thurlow didn't think.

"He had suspicions for years about Archer and had moved his legal paperwork elsewhere in the last few months before he died. His was a natural death, before you ask. His heart just gave out."

"I know. I think he had grieved too much for Mom and just couldn't go on any longer without her." Ayron wiped at her eyes, tired of crying. "But why was Archer here, pretending to be my lawyer? He knew that he wasn't."

"We know, love." Meg sat beside her, an arm around her. "That's what the investigators are working through. But Thurlow did manage to find out some more information this morning after the conference call. I think that's what he wants to talk with you about."

"But if Archer never left here, and I can't see him doing that, then who kidnapped us? Who forced us to marry?" Ayron stared at her rings and then shoved back from the table, running from the room. They could hear her steps on the stairs and then a door opening and closing quietly.

Everett watched from the hallway as Ayron shut the door before shaking his head. *Whoever was after this young couple,* he thought, *we need to find them and find them quickly. Eunice paused beside him.*

"Evan and Flannery are heading this way, Evan said. I don't know how we can reach Ayron."

"She's grieving in a lot of ways. She's also terrified. That's a given with what she was just told." Everett shook his head. "This is worse than what Evan and Flannery went through, and that was difficult enough."

Thurlow spoke from behind him, catching Everett's eye.

"She's with Tag?"

"She is, Thurlow. And you need to speak with her. You're heading out tonight?"

"We have to. Tully and I have commitments that we have to get to. Meg has appointments that she can't cancel. We don't want to leave, but we must." Thurlow moved to the door, stopping as Eunice spoke.

"She will send you away, Thurlow. She will want that. Ayron will not want any danger to come to you."

"I know, Eunice. But we need to be here or someone does." He turned when neither spoke. "Don't you agree?"

"We agree, but it has to be their decision. If Tag is not able to make that decision, then Ayron will make it for them. Until and unless the danger becomes clearer and closer, we can't do much." Eunice turned and walked away.

Chapter 24

Tag roused late that night or rather early the next morning, his eyes finally opened. He searched the room, lit only with a dim light. His eyes closed in thankfulness. He was home, he thought, before his eyes flew open once more and he shoved himself up to rest on shaking arms, searching for Ayron. A soft noise from beside him had Tag jumping and looking that way, fear briefly flickering across his face before he reached for Ayron.

Ayron clung to him, thankful that he was awake, but so afraid for him. He didn't hear the words that were hammered at him, lying unconscious on the floor of the cell as he had been. Ayron feared for his life. Archer had been specific as to what Tag faced. The rage that she had been party to had terrified her. Just how they were to stay safe, that she didn't know, but what she did know was that God was there. She had felt His presence in that cell and seemed to have caught sight of a man standing in the corner, that no one else seemed to see. She wondered at that.

"Ayron?" Tag's voice was hoarse. "You're okay?"

"I am, Tag." Sobs briefly shook her body. "And you're awake. You scared me."

"I did? I was so afraid for you." Tag sank back against the pile of pillows, his hand not releasing the one of hers that he had recaptured. "How did we get away?"

"Brownie. Someone came to him and told him where we were. We were there three days." Ayron was unable to stop the shudders of terror shaking her. "I thought that he had killed you."

Tag shook his head, regretting that movement. "He tried hard, but you know, I don't think he's the one behind it all. He was too careless. Did you hear him talking?"

It was Ayron's turn to shake her head. "I just sort of stopped listening to him. I guess that I shouldn't have?"

Tag gave a quick smile before he sobered. "No, I think you should have listened. I heard him on his phone, I think it was the second day. He was talking to someone and he was very subservient to that person."

"That doesn't surprise me, given what I know now." She reached for the glass of water, helping to hold it as Tag drank. "Your father did some digging. Apparently, Archer was no longer my lawyer even though he tried to pretend that he was."

"He wasn't? Your father had moved his legal stuff?"

"He had. Brownie said that the couple who tried to charge us? He's a relative of Archer's. That makes sick sense."

"It does." Tag sighed, his eyes dropping closed. "I'm sorry, my love. I just can't stay awake. Tell me that we're not on our own, that we have someone with us. I can't protect you and you need that."

Ayron watched as he slept, a deep sigh driven from her. "I can't tell you that, my sweetheart. I can't tell you that we are not alone. Because we are. Everyone has had to leave. Please, dear Lord, protect us this night, and heal Tag."

Moving slowly, Tag sank into the desk chair in the office the next morning. Ayron had walked behind him, her hands up to help him, but he hadn't seen her. She sighed. We are a married couple, but not a couple. And somehow, I don't think we will ever be. I don't think Tag meant what he said when he said that he wanted to stay with me. No one ever does.

Tag searched the desk, seeing the piles of paper and file folders before he reached for the concise briefing that his father had left him. Dad, thank you. This is what we need. Only I am too tired and in too much pain to even take in what you have said.

"Tag?" Ayron stood beside him, her hand resting on his shoulder. "I can go over what your father said."

"That would be good." Tag looked up, blinking to clear his vision. "So what did he say?"

"I told you earlier that Archer was not Dad's lawyer. That has been confirmed. The couple has been charged with fraud for her and fraud, trespass, and assault for starters for him. Archer has been taken away somewhere and I really don't want to know where. The owner of the farm where we were held is missing and we think dead."

122

"Dead? Buried on the farm?"

"We think so." Ayron watched as Tag thought through what she had said. "Tag? What are your thoughts?"

"That God provided for us. Sure, we went through some stuff." Tag stared at her. "That's not all, though, is it?"

Ayron shook her head. "No, it's not. Archer was determined that I marry him." She shuddered at that very thought. "I don't know who made us marry, but it had to be someone behind him. Your dad was working on that as was Evan. I don't know if they determined yet who is it."

"I see. Then, we'll see what we can do." Tag's eyes rested on the pile of material. "Did they leave all that?"

"Some of it. Emma has been sending information through as well. Ian called. He said that either himself or Joseph would be back through. He was muttering something about a security system?"

Tag grinned. "Joseph is the one on Abe's team who does that." Tag sighed as his grin faded. "I just can't do this, Ayron. I can't go through this material and I need to."

"Not today." Ayron drew him away from it. "You need to heal. You've had two brutal beatings in the last few weeks." She watched as he nodded and then headed for the back deck, sinking down into the swing and drawing her down with him, to wrap her into his arms.

"I know, my love. I know. It's just so difficult. I'm not one to sit back and this enforced rest does not work for me."

"Really? Who would have known?" She smirked at him before a thought crossed her mind. "Tag, who is this person really after?"

"I'm not sure I understand what you're saying." Tag watched her closely.

"I know that Archer was after me. But who kidnapped me and took me from here? It can't have been him. He would not have sent me your way. And it looks as if you were targeted, you know. So who are they after?"

Tag stared at her, realizing that she had just gone to the heart of the matter, the heart of what had bothered him. He had been targeted, that much he now understood. His father had discussed that with him when he was first released from the hospital. And he knew Eric was thinking that.

"I don't know, Ayron. I mean, I know people had resented me arresting them. There have been threats that have been made and traced back. I need to talk to Eric." He made to rise, only to find Ayron preventing him from doing that. "Ayron? I need to get up."

"No, you want to get up. You don't need to right now. I am sure that they are both working on that very thought. Tully was muttering something about it before he left."

Chapter 25

Two days later, Tag looked up in surprise as he heard the front door slam and then running footsteps. On his feet, he stared at Ayron as she burst into the room, terror on her face. She swept all the documents that he had spread out on the desktop into his arm and grabbed for the laptop, pulling the plug on the desktop computer before she was shoving him towards the secret room. Tag moved quickly, knowing that there was a reason, and turning as he heard thumping at the door.

The door slid closed behind them as Ayron dumped the laptop on the table in the room and then reached for the paper and folders to do the same. Tag reached for her, catching her into his arms, even as they heard movement in the office, and loud coarse voices. Her face burrowed against him as they stood, not sure if it was safe to leave.

Tag's voice was low in Ayron's ear as he whispered.

"What was that all about?"

Ayron still shook with fear. "It was that man. He was back. Only he wasn't on his own. Tag, what are we to do? I thought that he was locked up."

"He's made bail, more than likely, and come to find us. What is it about this house or property or you that they want?" Tag's voice was puzzled and Ayron could tell he was trying to come up with an answer.

"I have no idea. This was an ancestral home, that much I know, coming from Mom's side. Her grandfather built it." Ayron's voice slowed and then stopped. "He was a goldsmith, rare at that time."

"Do you think something has been hidden in the house? Have you searched?" He felt her head shaking against him.

"No, I never ever thought of that. Is that what this is about?" She frowned as she heard his phone chime. "Will they hear that?"

"I pray not." Tag reached for it. "It's Brownie. He's here and they have arrested that man, as you call him, and two others. He wants to know if we are safe and if we are to stay where we are until he calls us again."

Ayron sighed and then moved away from Tag, reaching for a light switch to turn on a low overhead light.

"Can we work on this while we're waiting? And what did you discover?"

Tag grinned at her. "Who said that I found anything?"

She spun to stare at him before her eyes narrowed. "I know that you did. I could see it before I headed for the door." Ayron paused. "That was just so strange. I headed for the door just to see what was going on. And I saw the car stop and that man get out and head for the door. I didn't know if we could make it into here."

"Locking the door likely slowed them down. I wonder if they went in the back door. He doesn't strike me as having a lot of smarts." Tag's attention was on the paper on top of the pile, one that he had not seen as of yet. "Ayron? This is in your handwriting. Who is this?"

Ayron peered over his arm at the paper. "Him? That's George's son, George Gordon Junior. He moved from here a number of years ago. There were rumours of a split in the family. Come to think of it, I don't remember seeing him around since he moved." Her face paled even more. "Is he the one?"

"The one who?" Tag finally looked up at her. "Ayron? What do you mean?"

"Him. George junior. Is he the one who made us marry? To get back at Archer? If Archer killed his father, then he would likely be out for revenge?"

Tag stared at her and then down at the paper before he reached for her laptop, signing in through the passwords that he needed to reach a secure site.

"What is his full name?" When Ayron didn't respond, Tag looked up. "Ayron, my love. What is the son's full name?"

"The same as his father." Ayron moved to stand beside him, a hand on his shoulder. "Do you really think that you can find him?"

"I do and I did." Tag sat back, frustrated. "It says that he was killed in a drunken-driving accident. He was drunk and drove off the road into a ravine. That was a number of years ago. That's why you haven't seen him."

"He was drunk?" Ayron paced before she spun to face Tag, who sat watching her. "His father was not a drinker. I never heard that George Junior was. How sure are we that he is dead? Could he have faked his death?"

Tag shook his head. "No, he was identified by his father. That is likely when his father just gave up. The run-down condition of the farm that you described doesn't just happen in a year or two."

"No, it doesn't. He was never the same." Ayron began to pace again. "You know, it has been rumoured that Archer had a son that he was estranged from. I don't remember him at all. But the rumours were that Archer had never married the woman and that she was very resentful of that. That she refused to let the son come around."

"Do you know his name?"

Ayron shook her head. "I never heard. As I said, it was all rumours. Maybe your Dad could come up with something." She moved to sit on the table, shoving over all the paperwork. "Tag, can I ask you something?"

"Sure." He sat back in the chair, his eyes on her.

"What are you planning on doing? With your health the way it is right now, can you continue as an officer?"

Tag sighed. Once more, she had gone directly to the heart of the matter. He loved that about her and only wished their relationship was such that he could tell her.

"I not likely will go back. I'm off on sick leave right now. Eric wants me to talk to someone, and I will. Right now, I am just trying to heal physically. This last episode has not helped."

"No, it hasn't." Ayron wrapped her hands around the edge of the table, lost in thought. "There are times that I wish I could just leave, run away where no one could find me, and then hopefully return at some point to find this all over. I don't see what God has in purpose for this."

Tag smiled. "I know, my love. I know. I feel the same. If I could escape to some deserted island with you until this was over, I would. A friend, Murphy, in fact, has a saying that God has a plan and purpose that we don't know about. I have to agree with him. I've seen it over the years."

Chapter 26

Brownie wandered through the rooms on the main floor of the house, disturbed that his friends had been terrorized again. And he could find no other word for it than that. He sighed. There was talk of finding somewhere to stash Tag and Ayron to keep them safe but he highly doubted that they would go. Tag would likely go on the run first, and that could get them killed.

Ayron watched Brownie before she turned and walked away, heading for the outdoors and her swing. She needed to think but more than that, she needed to pray. She sought her prayer corner and did just that. She didn't see Tag standing on the porch, watching her, his heart on his face, before he turned and sought Brownie.

"Brownie? Where do we stand?" Tag planted himself in front of Brownie, his eyes hard with worry.

"Not where we should be. Archer's cousin showing up like this has complicated everything. What have you two decided to do?"

"We're not running, if that's what you're asking. I'm not up to it physically. I have to go back south at some point, and have absolutely no desire to."

"This has become home." Brownie nodded at the look that crossed Tag's face. "Your lady love is here, Tag. She would move for you, but you won't ask her. Have you thought of what you want to do, then?"

Tag shrugged. "Dad has said that I could work for him. I don't think that I can ever go back to policing. The trauma has affected me too much."

"And that it is. You are a victim of crime, Tag. Just like all those people that we help. You need to heal in so many ways."

Tag sighed. "I know I do. So does Ayron. Listen, while we were waiting, we discovered something about her past. Her great grandfather was a goldsmith. Could that be related to what is happening today? That there is a hidden treasure here on the property somewhere?"

Brownie stared at him before he nodded. "Those are the rumours that have gone around for years. Ayron's people were too well thought right back to then for much credence to be given to that rumour. But I can see someone like Archer convincing himself that it was true." Brownie paused, deep in thought for a moment. "George's son? He left town years ago."

"He's dead. I found that out. He was killed driving drunk."

"That rules out him. But who would be related to Archer?" Brownie rubbed at his forehead. "I have no idea."

"Search for the one you least expect." Ayron spoke from behind him. "That's what Dad always said. The least obvious. Or the most obvious, one that you think was being set up or just couldn't be the one."

"He's right, Ayron." Brownie turned to watch her. "But we need to keep you two safe. Just how do we do that?"

Ayron kept her eyes on Tag, seeing his acceptance of and support for any decision that she would make.

"I'm not running, Brownie. Not one step. We do have to go down south for a couple of days, Tag needs that. Everett and Eunice are taking us. We didn't ask, they offered."

"I see. Okay, then." Brownie's eyes shifted between the pair. "That works. Ayron, what are you planning on doing? I know that you quit your work. Any reason why?"

Ayron shrugged before she began to pace, her hands reaching for different ornaments or books. She paused at a picture of her parents, taken on their wedding day, a hand reaching to brush away a tear. She didn't see the look on Tag's face as he took in her look.

"I don't know what I want to do. I didn't want to work there any longer. I can't explain it. He changed, you know? I would find him watching me, watching me in a way that made me uncomfortable. Dad and I had talked and he agreed that I should find something else. I had put in my resignation by the time that Dad went. He talked me into waiting for a couple of months, telling me that I didn't know what I was doing, that I was making a decision that was rash and emotion led." Ayron turned, a thoughtful look on her face. "He did change, Brownie, after that and just before. How is he related to Archer?"

Brownie's hand froze where he was rubbing it on his neck and his eyes slid closed.

"I don't think anyone ever asked you about that, did they? And we should have. I have no idea if he is related to Archer or not."

"What was his name, my love?" Tag moved to wrap her in his arms, his chin on her head as she responded by wrapping her arms around him.

"His name? Steve Arthurs. His family has been here almost as long as mine. In fact, I think they were all part of founding the village as it was." She spun in Tag's arms to face Brownie. "Is he involved?"

"I would suspect somehow he is." Brownie was at the desk, pointing to the material. "Can I look through that? In an unofficial capacity?"

Ayron shrugged. "Sure. Why not? If it helps solve whatever it is that we are involved in, go for it."

Tag moved to help Brownie search. Ayron watched before she glanced at the clock and knew they needed to eat.

Tag finally sat back, his finger tapping on a paper.

"Emma found this. She ties Arthurs with Archer. They are related, cousins of some standing."

"She does? I would like to know how she does that." Brownie reached for the material. "She's right, you know. They are related. And with the aliases that she has given for both, I recognize some of them. We have been looking for these men without knowing that they were right in our town. That's how well hidden they have kept."

———

"So, why force us to marry then? Revenge against her father? A division among thieves? An accountant would be a perfect cover for crime. I've seen it in the past."

Chapter 27

A week later, Ayron rose from where she had been working in the garden, brushing off her hands. She stopped moving as she saw the woman behind her.

"How did you get here? You're trespassing."

The woman, Arthurs' wife in fact, sneered at her.

"Not at all, my dear. I have the paperwork here for you to sign. You're signing over this house to us."

"No, I don't think so. I can't, even if I wanted to." Ayron's eyes rose as she saw Eric and Tag approaching her. "But there are some gentlemen behind you who really want to speak with you."

"There are not." Kit Arthurs screamed as Brownie fitted the handcuffs on her, causing the papers that she had held to fall to the ground.

Tag studied Kit, studied the papers, and then studied Ayron, a spark of mischief lighting his eyes.

"Can't leave you on your own, my love? You just go ahead with an adventure on your own."

Ayron's eyes narrowed as she caught the smile he was trying hard to hide.

"No, you can. It's just that other people decide I need an adventure when I really don't. Brownie,

---

please remove her and those papers that she seems to think I need to sign."

"Gladly, Ayron. Can you stay out of trouble for a bit? I'll be back." Brownie's grin at her lit up his face even as she sputtered at him.

Tag turned her to the house, stopping as he saw Brownie on the ground, the woman released and both Archer and Arthurs standing in front of them. He shoved Ayron behind him and began to back up.

"When we get close to the gate, run. I'll be behind you." Tag kept them moving, his eyes watching, listening for any sound of someone behind them.

Ayron turned her head to watch their progress, her hand clutching at the blue plaid shirt Tag was wearing. It was a warm day and she was in her bare feet. How did she run, she asked herself? But she knew that she would do just that. In fact, she knew exactly where she would run to.

"Run!" Tag's voice lashed at her even as he pulled the gate open, slamming it behind them and reaching for her hand.

"This way. I know a way that we can get away. If we have a few seconds, that is." Ayron pulled Tag with her down a little worn path, stopping just long enough to pull the branches back in place. She could hear Arthurs and Archer following them, their argument loud in the air.

Tag pulled her to a stop, leaning against a building, breathing hard.

"Just where are we?"

Ayron watched behind her, not confident that they had escaped.

"We're near the downtown area. Just a few buildings from the police detachment." Ayron reached for his hand. "Let's go. Brownie needs help."

"He does, but so do we." Tag followed her up the few stairs, horror on his face as he realized that she was barefoot. "Ayron, you have no shoes on."

"No, I don't but that doesn't matter. Brownie does."

Their sudden appearance startled the officers on duty before some were out of the door, heading for Ayron's place, the others moving the young couple away from the front of the building. The detective assigned to their case appeared and then sent someone for a basin of water and bandages. Tag took them with thanks and worked on Ayron's feet, even as they spoke with the officers.

Ayron breathed a sigh of relief as she saw Brownie in the doorway.

"Brownie?"

"It's okay, Ayron. I was blindsided by Arthurs. They are both arrested. How Archer made it back here, I would like to know."

"We'll find out. But if they're working together, who is the other party? The one who seems to be working against them?" Ayron's question dropped into the sudden stillness of the room, leaving all eyes to stare at her and then at one another.

Chapter 28

Thurlow stared at his son the next morning. He had appeared without warning, a sense that Tag was in trouble driving him to come.

"You said what?" When Tag repeated himself, Thurlow shook his head. "He showed up back here? He was not to be released at all."

"Well, he was." Ayron's disgruntled voice spoke from behind Thurlow. "And just how come you're here? We were to be going to you."

"I know, Ayron. A sense that you two were in trouble drove me to come. I have spoken with Eunice and Everett. We'll still make the trip down tomorrow. They are willing to come as well. Then we go from there."

"How sure are you that it is someone after me?" Ayron's question broke through the silence that had followed Thurlow's words. "Could it be someone after Tag?"

"It could be, and that we are trying to determine. It seems, son, that you have crossed paths at some point with Archer without knowing that you had."

"I have?" Tag's brow furrowed as he thought it through. "I don't remember him at all."

"No, I didn't think you had. Do you remember that accident you investigated a couple of years ago?

Where all those teens were hurt?" At Tag's nod, Thurlow sighed. "Tully and I have been looking into Archer. One of the younger teens was his grandson. He was left crippled. Archer has somehow blamed you for that. That's what we're hearing. but there is more to it than just that."

"There has to be. I remember that. I can't discuss it, but I was not the investigating officer. I was on the sidelines of it, directing traffic. So how does blaming me work?"

"That we don't know. I have spoken with Eric and he has asked the investigator to look into that. But that doesn't explain it at all." Thurlow was genuinely puzzled. "Ayron, we're looking into your family and your history. We are looking at Archer and Arthurs and their families. We are just not finding a link to the other party."

"And somehow, I don't think you will. Not until it is too late. Did anyone ever search that property and who owns it?" Ayron walked away, frustrated and more worried than she cared to admit.

"She's right, Dad. Did we look into that at all?" Tag sank back into a chair, exhausted. He just didn't seem to be getting any better.

"Tag? Have you been taking your pain medications?"

Tag nodded. "But all they seem to be doing is making me more tired." His eyes shot to his father. "They got to them, didn't they? Somehow, they got to them."

Thurlow gave a grim look and then a nod. He was away, back in a few minutes with the pill

———

containers in his hands, Ayron at his heels, questioning him as to just why he needed them.

"Tag? Are these the ones that you have been taking?" Thurlow handed them to his son.

Tag squinted at the bottles, his headache worsening. "They are, Dad. Why?"

Ayron reached for them. "No, that's not what was prescribed and that I picked up for him. Not even what he was given down south for the headaches. Who switched them?"

Thurlow sighed. "Someone has been in your home once more, doing this. Tag, we need to move you two somewhere else."

Ayron stared at him, and then her head began to shake.

"Absolutely not. I am not moving from my home. Tag can do what he wants to." Ayron was gone and they heard the door closing behind her.

"Tell me that she just didn't walk out the door." Tag was on his feet, heading after her.

"She did. And she has been stopped. I don't know who that is, though, Tag."

Tag peered through the door and then smiled.

"That would be Storm. A friend from another force. And Abe's Nathaniel and Matt. I wonder what news they have. It is odd that the three of them appeared together."

Storm looked up as Tag approached, an arm around Ayron.

"Storm? You're here."

"I am. I had to drop off something for you. And then I'm on my way." He handed over a parcel to Tag. "Call me at some point, Tag." He was gone before Tag could say anything.

Ayron stared after him. "Did he do that? Just hand you that and walk away?"

Tag grinned. "That's Storm, my love. But if you need to hide anywhere, he would find a spot for you. Or we could just call Ian. He'd fly us somewhere no one would ever find us.

Nathaniel and Matt broke out into laughter, startling Ayron, who stared at them in shock and then puzzlement.

"He would at that." Matt took pity on Ayron. "He offers to fly any lady in distress to an unknown location until we find the culprits."

"That he does." Nathaniel grinned at her. "By the way, I'm Nathaniel, that's Matt, and we both work for Abe."

"I sort of gathered that." Ayron sighed. "And no, we do not want any security people."

Abe's men continued to laugh as they followed Tag to the house, stopping to greet Thurlow.

"Where would you like to meet, Tag?" Matt held up a briefcase. "Emma's sent more for you."

Chapter 29

Matt watched Ayron for a while, later that afternoon, before he rose and approached her, sitting near her. Ayron heard the footsteps approaching her and looked up, startled, her eyes huge with fear. Matt sighed. *Tag, what do we do with you two?*

"Matt?"

"Ayron? You have a question?"

"I do. Flannery said that your team, as she called it, went in and found her and Lydia, I think she said. You found them and brought them home. I don't understand."

"Our team does training now for security teams. At one time, that's what we did. We went in and found people and brought them to safety. We provided security for VIPs and others who needed it. Just like you and Tag."

"Oh, okay. I didn't really understand." She peeked past him at where Tag sat slumped in a chair. She could tell that he was in pain. "Do you all do the same thing on the team?"

"No. I'm a paramedic, so I train in first aid. Nathaniel is our sniper and has never had to do that. He trains in how to find cover and what to expect and plan for that way. Why?"

"Oh, okay. I wondered. I am worried about Tag. His headaches are not getting better. We discovered this morning, just before you two appeared, that his medications are not what he should have been getting."

"We had that happen to one of our ladies. Someone had tampered with her medications. Has he seen anyone?" Matt shifted to watch Tag as well.

"He refuses to. We need him to. I spoke with his supervisor a bit ago. If he hasn't seen anyone by the time we arrive in his town, then he will have to. It's part of his assessment on sick leave. He is just too focused on trying to protect me and solve what is going on." Ayron gave a cry and sprang towards Tag as he slumped towards the floor, Matt reaching him first and laying him flat.

Thurlow reached for his phone, calling for help, then stood, his arm around Ayron, watching as Matt and Nathaniel worked on Tag. Nathaniel stepped back as the paramedics arrived.

"Nathaniel?" Thurlow's voice held worry.

"He's unconscious, Thurlow, as you can tell. I don't know much. We'll take you to the hospital." His hand raised, Nathaniel stared Ayron down. "We need to. This could very well be a setup to get to you, Ayron. Make Tag sick enough that he collapses and that leaves you vulnerable."

Ayron's hands covered her mouth before she moved to speak with the paramedics, fear on her face for Tag. Thurlow moved with her, Nathaniel and Matt flanking them, heading them out for their vehicle and then following the paramedic rig as it moved away rapidly.

Ayron paced the waiting room, not seeing the man standing at the entrance, his eyes focused on her. Matt and Nathaniel exchanged a glance before Nathaniel moved to stand behind him, just outside the door. Matt's feet carried him to pace with Ayron.

Brownie stopped beside Nathaniel, puzzled for a moment.

"Nathaniel, is it? Abe said that you were here. What's going on?" Brownie kept his voice low.

"He is. He's been focused on Ayron, and I don't like the way that he is watching her. He is also armed and unless he has reason to be, shouldn't have a weapon."

Brownie nodded and then tilted his head to study the man.

"Well, what do you know? We've been looking for him for another reason. Stay with me, Nathaniel." Brownie looked around, motioning for another officer to approach with him.

Brownie walked up behind the man, a hand on the man's shoulder keeping him in place. A few quiet words with him and the man nodded at last, realizing that he had been caught and that his life was likely forfeit at this point. He had failed.

Ayron frowned at the slight commotion before she turned to Matt.

"What was that all about?"

"That? Someone was watching you, Ayron. Brownie took care of it."

Ayron sighed. "We are making so much work for Brownie. He'll be glad to see the back of us."

Matt laughed, his eyes on Nathaniel who stood with Thurlow.

"Not likely, Ayron. Not likely. He's a friend and will stick with you both."

"I know. I didn't tell you that I was in school with him. We hung around in a group at school and then at church. Tell me, Matt. Where is God in this?"

"He's here, Ayron. He has kept both of you alive. He's working this out for you, for His glory. Sarah and I went through stuff, almost losing one another. So did Nathaniel and Elizabeth. She had someone stalking her for years. They went through a lot but came through with God's help. All of us did, as did a few of our friends. God is beside you, Ayron. Even though you can't see Him and at times doubt that He is, He has promised never to leave us or forsake us." Matt nodded towards the physician heading her way, Thurlow coming to stand beside her. "He is in the hands of the physicians treating Tag."

"Ayron?" The physician, Douglas Whitman, paused. "Tag is your husband? I hadn't heard that you had married. You didn't tell us." He grinned at her, a friend of long standing.

"It's no secret, Doug, but there's a story there." Ayron looked past him. "Tag?"

"We're doing some imaging on him. I understand that he has been beaten a couple of times?"

"He has been the first time, he was unconscious for how long, Thurlow? This is his father, Douglas, Thurlow Rafferty."

"About a week or so, Ayron. He went home before we really wanted him to but he was that worried about you, we just couldn't keep him in. We found out as well, Doctor, that the medications he had been given for pain had been tampered with." Thurlow pulled the containers out of his pocket. "This is what he had been taking. I need to give these to Brownie or the investigator."

"I see." Douglas took a look at the names. "That would do it. Now that we know what he has been taking and what he hasn't been taking, then we can see what we can do. He should be back from the CAT scan in a little bit, Ayron. I'll have one of the nurses come to find you."

Chapter 30

Tag stared at his father, seated in the front passenger's seat of his father's truck, hearing Ayron laughing softly behind him. There was no way that he had collapsed like that. He felt fine, he kept insisting.

"I am sorry, Tag, but you did faint or whatever it is you want to call it. Matt was there and he can verify it, if you really do doubt us."

"You did, Tag. We spent hours in the hospital with you. Don't you remember?" Ayron's voice held amusement, knowing that Tag was likely hiding the fact that he was well aware of what happened.

"I did, I guess. You said I was taking the wrong medication? How did I manage that?" Tag shifted to watch his bride.

"We don't know. Brownie said the investigator is working on that." Ayron's brow furrowed. "You know, he doesn't seem to be making much progress. We haven't heard from him in days."

"I know. I asked Brownie about that. He didn't say much." Tag leaned his head back on the headrest. "And what was that you said about Nathaniel?"

"Nathaniel found one of the men after us. He was standing in the waiting room watching me. He and Brownie just walked right up to the man." Ayron was puzzled over that. "Thurlow, what are we expecting to find in your hometown?"

"Answers, we hope. Safety for you two, we pray. Eric will be around tonight, Tag. He's tied up in court, he said. The investigator here is forging ahead, finding information that should have been found years ago. It looks as if you were a target, Tag, you and Ayron both. He's connecting the dots as they say. He hopes to have some good information that he can share in a day or so."

"And we will be here that long?" Tag was getting restless. He didn't do illness very well, never had, and this was testing him past the limits of his endurance. He wanted it over so that he could start a life with Ayron, that was, if that was her wish.

Meg watched as Tag stood on their front steps, not moving towards the door, his eyes on Ayron. She sighed. No, he really doesn't want to be here, but he should be here. We need to step back. Meg turned to Thurlow, finding him beside her.

"We need to let them move to his place, my love." Thurlow spoke her thoughts out loud.

"I know we do. Only, how safe will they really be?"

"I don't know. It doesn't appear that they are safe anywhere right now."

Tag turned Ayron back to face the street, walking that way with her, her hand tight in his.

"I think we need to go home, my love. Not here. Your home. It's ours now."

"No, it's mine. Yours is here." Ayron was puzzled at Tag's words.

Tag shook his head. "Wherever you are, Ayron, that's my home. I am in love with you, more every day. Only I don't know how you feel. If I need to set you free, then I will."

Ayron studied him, and then the road. "So, how do we get to your place?" She looked up as a car stopped. "Everett?"

Everett grinned at her. "I know. You want to go to Tag's. Hop in, and we'll take you there. Your parents understand."

"They do? How would they know?" Ayron turned back to the house, finding Thurlow and Meg standing a few feet behind them. "We can't just walk away from here."

"You can, Ayron. If that's what you two have decided to do, we accept that. We don't want to hover, but we do want to protect you. Sometimes protecting a person is letting them go." Meg reached to hug her daughter-in-law. "This is what you need to do. We are close, only a phone call away. Go to Tag's, dear. We'll do a conference call tonight if we have to."

Tag pulled her with him, walking past Everett's vehicle and heading for a nearby park. He needed to talk with her, without anyone else around, and that he had to do then.

"Tag? You just walked away from your parents!"

"I know." He looked around, finding a bench and drawing her down and into his arms. "We need to talk, Ayron. And talk now."

"About what?" Ayron refused to look at him.

"About this, whatever this is that we are involved in. Dad has gotten too involved. I can't get him to stop or back away at all. And he needs to. Everett and Eunice will get involved as will Evan and Flannery. How well do you know the investigator in Lakeside?"

"I don't know him. But I don't trust him. I've been afraid to tell Brownie that. It's a small force and they don't have many investigators."

"That's what I have been picking up from you, then. Your reluctance to meet with him and his reluctance to come around us. He should be back asking questions, finding information, and he's not. Brownie is doing that and shouldn't be."

"That's what has me puzzled. Would Emma look into him and see if he has any connection to Archer or Arthurs or someone who is evil?"

Tag grinned at her words. "She can. I asked her that on our way down. She sent me a text to tell me that Jace, who works for her, is doing that. They had already had that thought."

"This just keeps getting better and better." Ayron grew silent, not aware of how much Tag was keeping watch and didn't see the patrol officer heading their way, nodding at Tag as he took up a position near them. Eric had been called and sent him to watch out for them. Tag would have told her that God was in that.

Chapter 31

Tag wandered his house. Ayron had already retired and he knew that he should but something was off and he wasn't sure what. He searched, a sigh rising from him as he found the cameras and microphones. This was not how he wanted it. Someone had breached his security system and he would love to know just how they had done that.

Hours later, Tag turned from the door, to sink down on the couch, his head hitting a pillow had placed there, too tired to even reach for a blanket. His friends had been through, finding what he had found, questioning him as to why. Tag had shrugged, simply asking what the word on the street was. He had not liked what he had heard, that someone was seeking for someone to kill him. And Tag knew why, or so he thought. He had stepped in with Ayron, even forced as it was, and that someone wanted him out of the way. Only Tag had no idea why.

Ayron had paced his house before she had retired, a frown on her face. Tag had stood, a shoulder against a doorframe watching her, before she planted herself in front of him.

"Tag? Where are the packages? The letters? The threats? We're not getting them. Your medication was tampered with. But shouldn't we be getting warnings of some kind?"

"We should, my love, and we're not. Eric mentioned that. It has us puzzled. It makes me think that whoever it is that is behind all this is keeping a very close watch on us and knows exactly where we are and who we are with."

"I don't like that thought." Ayron had moved into his hug. "Tag? Can we disguise ourselves and run away? Hit the streets and hide there? Don't you know some undercover or street cop that could help us?"

Tag had begun to laugh as she spoke, knowing that she was grasping at straws.

"I do know a few, my love. If I thought it would help, then I would do just that. But for now, how be you head off for bed? It will be a long day for you tomorrow, what with me in medical appointments."

"And I intend to go with you." She leaned back. "I can't not do that, Tag. No matter what our decision is when this is all over, I have to be there for you. They would expect that, now wouldn't they?"

"They would." Tag paused, a thought hovering at the edge of his thoughts, not quite clear enough to express. "We need to talk about that."

"We will. Good night, Tag." Ayron felt his kiss on her cheek before she moved away. She just wished that she knew who it was and could confront them. But then, confrontation usually meant harm or death, and she was just not ready for that. Her prayer was for safety, that God's promises would be true for them. She was seeking for her refuge and her hiding place and to know God in a deeper way. Only this was not how she ever expected to be doing that.

Covering Tag with a light blanket early the next morning, Ayron's hand rested on his cheek, feeling the stubble on it, and seeing the lines of pain and worry and stress that were etched there, lines that she felt were her fault. She turned at last, heading for the kitchen, finding food and coffee, a mug of coffee in her hand as she stood staring out the living room window. She felt caged and suddenly wondered if that was the aim of whoever it was. To cage her and then destroy her. She prayed for wisdom, suddenly realizing that whoever it was, it could well be a female. That scared Ayron, knowing how devious and dangerous women could be.

Tag had risen quietly and then showered, shaved and in clean clothes, he too had reached for a mug of coffee, coming to stand shoulder to shoulder with Ayron. He was quiet, just letting her had her silence. His head felt clearer than it had in days, but he still had a decision to make, one that he felt unready to do.

"Tag? How sure are we that it is a man after us?"

"We're not. Emma said that she thought it was a female. I tend to agree with her. This had never made sense from a male point of view. She has a friend who has done a profile for her and she has passed it on to Eric. For some reason, she has refused to give it to the investigator in Lakeside."

Ayron sighed as her head rested against Tag, thinking that she was doing a lot of that lately.

"I know the investigator now. I know his connection to the Arthurs. His parents were good

153

friends of theirs. He is likely not working for us, delaying everything."

"We need to talk with Eric then."

"I sent him a text late last night. I haven't heard back from him. What was going on last night? I heard voices other than yours."

Tag nodded, sipping at his coffee before he spoke. His eyes studied the parking lot, narrowing as he watched a vehicle slowly circling the lot multiple times.

"I found cameras and microphones here. Someone has got in past my security system. I have a call in to that company and they are to get back to me. What you asked me about not happening? It seems as if it is now. They had time to prepare for us to come back."

Ayron drew in a deep breath. "What are your plans, Tag? Can you continue as an officer? I know that you are off on medical leave but at some point, they will want an answer."

"I know that they will. I am not sure. It depends on how well I heal. But I find that I like a little town called Lakeside. It has potential. I can see a drop-in centre or resource centre there, for anyone who needs it. I have been doing research as to grants and start-up costs."

"You have? And you didn't tell me?" Ayron turned to him. "Is that what you want to do?"

Tag shrugged. "I am not sure. Evan is involved in a camp that his father started up for teens in trouble and they have a home that is near them for anyone who needs it."

"I think that is a wonderful idea. What I have always wished we had in town was just that. A centre to help, with people paying as they can, and free if they can't. Times are changing. People are moving in and out of town. There has never been anything like this."

"We'll think about it. Pray about it. Seek counsel on it. But for now, I need to get moving for an appointment. I am still not cleared to drive. Can you drive a truck?"

"I can. Dad had one." Ayron frowned. "And it has not been returned. Just where is it?"

Tag froze. "It hasn't been? I didn't realize that. I thought you didn't need a vehicle. Does Brownie know?"

Ayron shrugged. "I would gather that he does and is working on that. I spoke with the insurance company a couple of days ago. They were putting in a report to the police."

Chapter 32

Her hand tight in Tag's, Ayron listened quietly as the medical examiner that Tag had been asked to see spoke with him. She frowned at his words.

"Do you understand what I am saying, Tag?" The physician's kindly eyes watched Tag closely.

"I do. You said that you don't think I am ready to return to patrol any time soon. Given the beatings, the abuse that I took, the headaches, it is just too risky." Tag glanced at Ayron. "It's what Ayron and I have discussed. I understand that."

"I don't know that you will ever be able to return. For now, I am signing you off on long-term disability. We will need to meet again in about six weeks. You have a physician in Lakeside?"

"We do. I spoke with my own physician. He will take Tag on." Ayron rose as Tag did, a frown on her face as they walked out of the building. "Someone is watching us, Tag. Where are they?"

"I know. I have no idea where they are. I know that someone has put out a hit on me, just because we're a couple. And I would like to know why." Tag was getting angry.

"I know. So would I. How do we find out?" Ayron slid behind the wheel of the truck. Tag was not allowed to drive for another week. "And when do we go back north?"

"As soon as we can. We'll pack up my house. The lease is due to be signed in the next week or so. I can give it up easily. My heart is no longer here in this town." Tag didn't see the look Ayron threw him, his attention outside, watching for just who, he wasn't sure.

"Are you sure, Tag? Your family and friends are here."

"They are, but you're not. You're not ready to leave your town. You may never be. I am content to move there, my love. And we will talk." Tag watched as the car behind them crept closer and closer. "Ayron, there's a parking lot here on the right. Turn into it and keep going, behind the stores. There's a street there I want you to turn onto."

She stared at him for a brief moment before looking in the rearview mirror. "I see. We have a tail, do we? Okay. Now where?" She followed his instructions, heading for a building across town. "What is this place?"

"It's a hideaway that we have. I need to call this in and this is as good a place as any for us to wait." He was out of the truck and reaching for her hand as she opened her door. "We can get a meal in a small restaurant here, head back for the apartment and start packing. I have a friend who is a mover, who offered to help."

Tag tucked Ayron back into the truck, turning as he heard his name called. A patrol officer was walking towards him, hand out to shake Tag's.

"Tag? What have you gotten involved in?" Tom shook his head. "We pulled the car over. Found a lot of interesting articles. As well as a paper with your name and address on it."

"I know, Tom. There's a hit out of me, I'm told, and I have no idea why." Tag angled his body to watch Ayron. "And I fear for Ayron."

"Ayron?" Tom's gaze shifted towards the truck. "The lady driving your truck?"

"That's Ayron. She's my bride." Tag drew a deep breath, ready to continue when Tom raised a hand.

"We heard, Tag, and wondered. What can we do for you?"

"Right at the moment? I'm packing up and moving to Lakeside, Ayron's hometown. For now, anyway. I haven't made any further decisions. I'm off on disability."

"And you're not sure if you will ever return?" Tom's face grew grim. "Who?"

"We don't know, but Ayron's former lawyer tried to sell her house. Cleared it out in fact. Ayron's in the process of getting her home back in order. She's not ready to leave her hometown."

"And you won't make her. Let me have your address there. I'll round up some fellows and yes ladies to help you pack. Knowing you, that's happening today."

"It is. I fear for Ayron. She lost her father not that long ago, was kidnapped, driven around the province, and then forced to marry me. I couldn't let them kill her." Tag's face and voice were sober.

"Not even if it meant leaving the work you love. We get that Tag. We're behind you." Tom shifted his body, to stare at the street. "I'm off in a couple of hours. I'll head your way. And I will bring a meal."

"Thanks, Tom. Appreciate it."

"Go, get in your vehicle. I'll follow you home." Tom waited for Ayron to pull away before he followed, his eyes watching the car behind him. Another one, Lord? Another tail. His call to their dispatch brought another patrol vehicle to follow him, the officer pulling over the vehicle.

Ayron looked at him as she pulled into his parking spot, and then at the numerous men and ladies that were milling around.

"Brought in reinforcements?"

"My fellow officers, Ayron. Tom arranged that." He sighed, his eyes on her. "I'm sorry. I should have asked if you were okay with this."

Ayron shrugged. "I am. They're your friends. They want to spend time with you. I will not stop them." She shivered suddenly, fear driving through her. "Are we leaving here today?"

Tag shook his head, his hand on hers. "Not today. In the next couple of days. We can stay with Mom and Dad or find a motel."

Ayron nodded, a sober look on her face. "I hate this for you, Tag. I truly do. Your life has changed so much, just because of me, and we don't know why or who."

"Ayron, look at me." His eyes were steady on her as she did what he asked. "If I had to make the choice under any circumstance, I would still choose you. God has blessed me with you as my wife. We need to talk but you're not ready yet to hear what I want to say. I pray that it will be soon, but it is in God's timing."

Ayron studied the man that she had been forced to marry, seeing his character and hearing his words, hearing underneath them the longing and emotions that he was holding back. She sighed to herself. *Lord, I don't know about this. I know that You have allowed it but it's hard. So very hard. This is when I need my mom and dad and don't have either. Who do I go to for advice, that knows me?*

Chapter 33

Tag watched his friends as they sorted through his belongings and then helped the movers pack them into the moving van. He was saddened that his life as he knew it was over but he was also aware that he was in God's hands, that God had allowed this. He turned to find Ayron, seeing his mother standing with an arm around her, her head bent as she prayed for the younger woman.

Thurlow watched his son, his heart breaking for him, knowing that Tag was giving up a dream that he had had since a child, that of being a police officer. He smiled to himself as he thought back through the years, as Tag grew from a toddler, through his childhood, youth, and teens, into a young man who had proudly shown them his brand-new uniform, excited about starting a career that he felt God wanted him in. *Now,* Thurlow thought, *God was leading him into a different path in his life and that meant Tag was moving from their town. Not that he was going that far, but it would change for them. Tully had married and stayed in town, working for his father in his investigative office, but Tag?* Thurlow was having trouble reading his son for the first time.

"Dad?" Tully spoke from beside him. "What's Tag going to do now?"

"He said he's not sure. He's off on disability. I doubt that he will ever be able to go back."

"That's what we're afraid of. Listen, I'm heading that way next week. I want to do some research."

"Talk to Tag first before you go. He may have information for you. And Brownie has been in touch. He's worried about Ayron. They're old friends, he tells me, going through school together and involved in groups at their church."

Tag approached his father, just standing beside him, gazing around his house. It was hard to let it go, he decided, but it was so necessary.

"Tag? You okay?" His father's voice was low. "And what's this I hear about tails today?"

"Two of them, Dad. Tom looked after them for us. I don't get it. Who is doing this? We're no closer to finding out."

"No, we're not but we are working on it. Emma is feeding us information and so is Jace. Eric's been getting it and passing it on to whoever it needs to go to. Brownie's doing the same. We need to talk, son."

"Not today, Dad. Not today. I don't know when we will." Tag walked away from his father, his arms going around Ayron as she stood, hands on her face, staring around at the rapidly emptying house. "Ayron?"

"Tag? Are you really sure?" Ayron twisted to stare up at him.

"I am, my love. My home is where you are. Not here. You're not ready to leave there. We'll figure it out."

Ayron nodded, still saddened that Tag's life had changed that much. She leaned back on him, not realizing that she had, trusting him in a way that she didn't trust others. She heard his whispered prayer for peace for her, for strength, and for a resolution of what they faced. Ayron feared that, that resolution. She just knew that Tag would pack up and move away and she wasn't ready for him to do just that.

Meg watched her son, a hand rubbing at her arm. She was afraid for him, she thought. She had no idea what he was facing but God did. How did she trust Him to protect Tag? So far, Tag had been in so much danger. Meg knew his character, knew that he would not walk away from Ayron. Thurlow wrapped an arm around her.

"It's a hard road he has to walk, Meg, but God is there. He knows the path that we walk and the reasons for it."

"I know, Thurlow. I know. It doesn't help a mother's heart though."

Tag grinned at his mother, knowing her thoughts.

"We know, Mom. We know. Listen, we're all done here. Thanks for your help. Dad? I think we'll head out tonight. They would expect us to stay over."

"Are you sure, son?" Thurlow worried about the trip, knowing that it was late in the day.

Ayron and Tag shared a look. They had decided to leave and then stop before it got too late, if they wanted to. They felt danger approaching and Ayron was worried for his family.

———

"We are, Dad. Listen, thanks once again."

Ayron studied Tag late that night. She had insisted that they come home, or at least to her home. Tag, she really wasn't sure what his thoughts were. Tag wandered the house and then outside, searching. She sighed to herself. He was doing it again, she thought. Trying to protect her and they really didn't know from whom.

Brownie and Ella had both called. Brownie stated that the lawyer had been transferred elsewhere, to face charges of murder and extortion and what all, he wasn't sure. Ella had asked what she could do for Ayron and just laughed when Ayron had protested.

Tag stepped back through the door, locking it behind him, a thoughtful look on his face. He had spoken with Emma when he had been outside. She told him that she had found someone behind the lawyer and that man scared Emma. For her to admit that? Tag knew that she was. She hadn't said who yet but he knew it was coming. That meant more danger for Ayron, and just how was he to protect her? He continued to seek for answers, but they were not forthcoming. The only answer that he found when he sought the Lord was to wait, that God was in control, that they would not face anything that He didn't already know about and would get them through.

Chapter 34

Slamming the door in fear, Ayron searched for somewhere to hide. Tag was out somewhere, just where she wasn't sure. She ran for the secret room, sliding to a halt as she saw the man standing in front of her. Ayron backed away, desperate to escape, finding arms coming around her from behind and trapping her. She struggled to escape, unable to do that, bodily lifted and carried from her home. Thrown roughly into a camper, she spun, ready to fight, to run, stopping as she saw the knife held up in front of her.

"Stop fighting. You'll only get yourself killed. And he doesn't want that. Not yet." The man's snarl stopped her even as the door shut behind him and the second man moved towards the driver's seat. "Sit."

When Ayron refused to sit, her arm was roughly grabbed and she was thrown into a seat, handcuffs clicking around her wrists, and the seatbelt pulled around her and snapped closed. Her eyes searched for the house and for Tag, not seeing him around. Please, *Lord, keep him safe. Let him know that I do love him. I don't know that I am going to go home. Only You know that.*

An hour later, Tag stood in the kitchen, not finding Ayron anywhere in the house. He had searched the yard and garage and not found her. She hadn't left a note, not that he could see, and he remembered that she had been adamant that she was not going out. Tag turned as Brownie entered the kitchen.

"She's not here, Brownie. Not anywhere. Where is she?" Tag struggled with his emotions, knowing in his heart that whoever it was that was after them had her.

"We'll look. A neighbour mentioned a small camper down the road for a while when you were out. Their security camera picked it up. We have seen activity around it."

"Ayron?" Tag's eyes slid closed as Brownie nodded. "Who took her?"

"That we are working on." Brownie reached for his phone, sighing as he read the text message. "It's stolen, as we thought."

"Who? Who is it?" Tag felt the anger growing in him. He just wanted Ayron back, to hold her in his arms, and finally tell her that he loved her with all his heart and being, but that he loved her enough to set her free if that was her wish. *Lord, please? I can't do this. Not any more.*

Thurlow dropped his phone on his desk, turning as Meg touched his shoulder.

"Ayron disappeared. Tag doesn't know that Brownie called me." He sighed. "I can't head that way, not for a few days, and neither can Tully. We're too deep into that investigation."

"We ladies will head that way, then. We'll be fine." Meg moved away as the doorbell rang, opening to find Matt and Ian standing there, folders in their hands. "Matt? Ian? What brings you two here? Come in."

"Emma sent us. Is Tag here?" Matt's eyes raised to Thurlow's, a frown covering his face.

"No, Tag and Ayron headed home. The thing of it is? Ayron disappeared just a few hours ago. Tag was out and when he returned home, she was gone." Thurlow's shoulders slumped for a moment as he bent under the sorrow the two were facing.

"Gone?" Ian was moving back through the door, his phone out. "Abe? We're with Thurlow. He just received word that Ayron has disappeared today/"

"She has?" Ian could hear Abe's steps on the parking lot at their building. "That's what we were afraid of. Emma was picking up that."

"I know. Where do you want us?"

"Back here once you've finished with Thurlow. We have that group in for training starting tomorrow and we need all of us." Abe paused. "I can call in another team, but not without talking to Tag. And I don't think he'll go for that. Not with Ayron missing."

"I know. They're after him, and I just don't get why. How do Ayron and Tag connect? It can't be random."

Thurlow had approached Ian, watching as he tucked his phone away.

"Matt said you two had to head home."

"We do, as much as we would like to stay with you. We have that material for you that Emma sent. Let us know what we can do."

Thurlow sighed, his hands jammed into his pockets, his eyes on the trees in the distance.

"To tell you the truth? I am not sure any more what we can do. The ladies are heading that way, just to see what they can do and to be there for Tag."

"That's good. He needs family with him." Ian turned as Matt approached. "Call us, Thurlow, if there is anything we can do. Emma's sending Jace up there to speak with the investigators at some point over the next couple of days."

"Thank her for us." Thurlow watched as they drove off before he reached for his phone, turning it over in his hands, not sure what he should be doing.

Tag reached for his phone, a small smile on his face as he read his father's message. Yes, he thought, Mom would come, even though there is not a lot that she can do. Even as an adult, he acknowledged that there were times he just needed his mother.

Brownie watched Tag's face, a grimness to his. He had spoken with his chief and the word was not good. They had received a ransom demand for Ayron. Only it wasn't really so much a ransom demand as a demand for Tag to give himself up to them. And that they would not let happen, not if they could prevent it.

"Tag? Where was your investigation at?"

Tag turned, shrugging. "Not sure. Ayron was working on people in the town that she suspected. She may have left it on the desk or to a file on the computer." His steps were slow and heavy as he moved back into the house, Brownie's hand resting on his shoulder for a moment.

Chapter 35

Three days had gone by, three days with Ayron missing. Tag had finally be advised of the ransom demand and the refusal to go along with it. He had stared at the police chief, at Ella, and then at Brownie, his hands running through his hair before they rested on the top of his head. Tag had walked away, knowing that they were looking out for him, but it just didn't sit right with him. Their refusal to cooperate didn't bring Ayron home and just might mean that she never came home. Not alive. And that thought scared him more than anything had ever done, and he had seen way too much on his patrols, he thought.

Tag had not slept, at least not much, roaming the house and the yard, and then the town, searching for Ayron, and not finding her. The townspeople had watched in sympathy and then searched themselves. At least most of them had. There were a number who resented Ayron and her family. That had distressed Tag, who tried hard to hide his feelings from his mother, not quite succeeding.

Evan showed up in the late afternoon of the third day, his hand reaching to stop Tag's pacing.

"Tag? What can we do?"

Tag shrugged, his eyes on his friend. "How did you do it? When Flannery was missing? How did you do it? I know you coped. We've talked. But what can I do?"

"It's difficult, Tag, and different for each one. For me, I had a good idea where Flannery was but we weren't married. We were dancing around one another at that point, not sure how the other one felt. Now, about this? Who do suspect the least or suspect the most?"

Tag shook his head and then pointed at the kitchen table. "There. That's what I have come up with. Take a look at it. I don't know the people in this town and I'm guessing at that."

"Okay, so we take a look at it." Evan reached for the coffee pot, pouring both of the men's coffees, and then sat, pulling the paper towards him. "Is this just your work?"

"Mine and what Ayron had started. She was listing people in town, ones that she suspected and what she knew about them. She's good. Her mind works in a logical manner." Tag rubbed at his eyes. The fatigue and pain were catching up with him, and he wasn't thinking too clearly. He stared at the tabletop, his hands wrapped around his mug.

"Tag? Who is this? I don't think this person is from this town." Evan pointed to a name. "I remember him from our patrols. We always felt that he skirted the edge of the law and went over without any evidence to catch him."

"Which one?" Tag read the name and then Ayron's comments. "He is from this town. And I had dealings with his son and his son's friends. Is this why? Revenge?"

"It could be. Ayron notes that her father had dealings with him and had to have him charged, but I don't see that the charges went anywhere. Do you?"

"No, not that I can tell. We need to have someone look into this." Evan sorted through the paperwork. "Here. Emma has. And she has found so much on him. How did it ever get missed?"

"I don't know." Tag rubbed at his eyes again, unable to see clearly. "Brownie hasn't said much."

"No, I don't suspect he has. Do they have any clues as to where Ayron is?"

Tag shook his head. "None. He did say that there had been a ransom demand the first day but nothing since. That scares me, Evan. Is she even still alive?"

"They want you for something, Tag, and are using her to get to you. It's working. You're not sleeping. Not likely eating. Someone is close by watching you." Evan paused, a thought running through his mind. "What do you know about her neighbours?"

"I have only met the one next door, who she said was a friend. Is he involved?"

"Let me have his name." When Tag mentioned it, Evan's hand stilled, his eyes on the paperwork. "He's in her work, Tag. I think she is suspicious of him."

"I am. It didn't make sense, him saying that he was able to sneak in and put her computers in the secret room." Tag was on his feet, heading for the office, Evan following, a frown on his face. "In here.

This is the secret room. I don't get that her father would have told him, but he must have."

"Unless he searched the house and found it?" Evan stared in. "I don't like this, Tag. How do we know, as you say, that he had been told? It doesn't make sense that he could just sneak in when they were packing up the house."

Tag shook his head. "Can Dooley or Eunice look into him for us?"

"They can. Storm was asking about you when you were at your home. Did you give it up?"

"I did. The lease was due and I just didn't sign it. If I ever go back, I can find another place."

"But you don't want to." Evan walked around the secret room. "I wonder what this was for originally. Did Ayron ever say?"

"No, we never really talked about it." Tag stood, searching the room, his eyes rising to the top shelves. "It's strange that there is shelving in here." He left and returned with a small ladder, opening it and then standing on it to search the shelves. "Here, Evan. I found something." He handed down a roll of paper and then a small metal box. "I wonder if Ayron knew that these were here. They were as far back as they could get on the shelf."

"This is it? There's no more?" Evan's head tilted to watch Tag. "These ceilings are high."

"They are. Ayron said that they were nine feet high. An older home has that. I love it about her home."

Evan set the rolled paper down and frowned at it.

"Do we open it, Tag?"

"We have to. It may be what brings Ayron home. Although I doubt that." He reached for it, carefully unrolling it. "It's old, Evan, and fragile."

"What is that?" Evan's finger stabbed at it.

"A map. No, not a map, just made to look like one. I can't read it."

"I can't either. Who do we know that deals in this type of antiquities?" Evan looked up as Tag made a sound. "Tag?"

"Jacob Whitson. Remember him?"

"I do. I haven't thought of him for a long time. Why him?"

"He's married. His wife deals with stuff like this. He lives in Mistletoe." Tag reached for his phone, taking a photo of the parchment and then forwarding it to Jacob. "He'll have Finn take a look at it and then get back to me. But it doesn't answer the question of who and why?"

Chapter 36

Turning from the window that she had been staring out, Ayron studied the bedroom that she was captive in. She had no contact with anyone, her meals slid through a small opening at the bottom of the door. No amount of pulling or pushing had been able to budge the door. She had tried prying at the windows with the same result. Ayron sighed to herself. Held captive and not knowing why really didn't cut it, she thought. *God? Where are You? Is this how I am protected? Kidnapped and locked up? This has never made sense.*

A rattle at the door signalled the approach of someone. This was unusual, she thought. No one had been around her since she had been shoved roughly inside. Ayron kept her eyes on the window and the view that had become familiar to her. She heard footsteps stop behind her and waited, her eyes sliding closed as she heard the voice.

"Ayron, hiding your face from me won't work." Her next-door neighbour stood behind her. "You're not leaving here, you know."

"Why? Why did you do this?" Ayron fought to control the tremor in her voice, to control the deep fear or terror that she felt.

"Because. Just because. And Tag will come here. He will come to find you. He's not leaving either."

Ayron spun to stare at Terry. "I don't get it, Terry. You were Dad's friend."

"No, not really. I just pretended that."

"All your life? I don't get why."

"Easy. Your father had something I wanted and refused to give it up." He walked away, a cruel laugh trailing behind him. "And that something was you."

"Wait! You can't leave like that! Why me?" Ayron ran after him, too late to prevent the door from being slammed and the locks snapped on. "Why? Terry? Why? What did I ever do to you?" Ayron hammered at the door, getting no response, before she slid to the floor, fear running through her, as well as worry. *Lord, keep Tag safe. I can't handle it, knowing that he has been threatened.*

Tag turned as Brownie approached him at the back of the yard. He had been roaming it, not able to settle to anything. He had sent his mother and Lia home, telling them that they were needed there. That he would call if he needed them. He spoke daily with his father, who didn't say much other than to say he was praying for them.

Brownie sighed, knowing that Tag would not like what he had to say. Eric had been in touch. The investigator had been run down and critically injured in a hit and run. They suspected that it was related to Tag and Ayron but could not prove that.

"Brownie? I don't like that look." Tag paused in front of the gate.

"No, and you'll like what I have to say even more. Eric called."

___

176

"And?" Tag's attention was not fully on Eric.

"The investigator on your case was run down today. He's in critical condition."

Tag's gaze shot to Eric before he frowned. "And they don't know who or even if it's related to us."

"No, they don't. Eric's worried about you."

Tag shrugged and turned back to the gate. "It's a given that would happen. It doesn't explain where Ayron is."

"You're interested in that gate, Tag. Care to share why?"

"I am. It was open when I came out here a while ago. I don't see that anyone has been through it though."

Brownie's hand reached for Tag and pulled him back towards the house.

"Tag, in the house. That has been done on purpose, more than likely, to draw you outside there. You would disappear, the gate would be closed and we would have no idea where you were."

Tag nodded. "I know. But I still think I need to go through it and see what is out there."

"Not happening, my friend. In the house. Lock the doors. I know, you're a police officer but right now? You're the victim here, whether you want to acknowledge that or not. Just do what I ask, please?"

Brownie headed back for the house fifteen minutes later, a frown on his face. Someone had been there, that much he knew, but they were gone. And

Tag was still at risk. Brownie's eyes raised to the house and then he was running for it, the open door at the back catching his eye. He searched the house, not finding Tag, pausing in the kitchen, seeing the blood smeared on the floor that he had not seen on his way in. He reached for his phone. This was not what they needed, not at all. With Tag gone, how did they get Ayron back, let alone finding them?

Chapter 37

The man stood over Tag's body where it had been dropped onto the wooden floor. Tag had put up a fight, not surprisingly, the man thought, but it didn't help. He had had to resort to violence to put Tag down and he regretted that. His eyes raised as he stared at the door. Tag had information for him, that he more than likely didn't know about, and he needed that. The firm that he worked for was building a case against the man who they knew was involved in the situation that both Tag and Ayron found themselves in, without knowing why.

The man left and then returned, kneeling beside Tag and reaching to roll him to his back. His hands reached for the water in turn, wringing out a cloth and wiping at the blood. This was not good, he thought. Tag shouldn't have fought him, but he had refused to do what he had been asked, instead going on the offensive.

Tag groaned as he roused, feeling the gentle hands on his head. He squinted against the light, not sure where he was or exactly what had happened.

"Tag?" The man's voice was quiet. "Can you sit up?"

Tag nodded, regretting it as the headache pounded for a moment. The man's arm braced him from behind before he has raised to his feet and then to a chair, his hand wrapped around an open bottle of water.

"Here. Take these. It will help your headache. Once it's eased, we need to talk."

Tag squinted once more at the man, feeling that he really should know him.

"Who are you? And where am I? And did you really have to hit me?"

"I regret that, Tag. But you just won't listen to me." The man walked away, across the floor to the kitchen, where he stood, his stance watchful, even as he reached for the loaf of bread on the counter and then for meat and cheese to make their supper.

Tag took a deep drink of water, studying the room he was in. A cabin, he thought, a nice cabin.

"Where am I? And why?"

The man returned to stand in front of Tag before he handed him a plate, setting a mug of coffee beside him. He headed back to the kitchen to fetch his own dinner, trying to sort through his thoughts. Tag had thrown him off when he resisted.

Tag thought back to the fight that he had tried to avoid but had been unable to. Then, he frowned. *No,* he thought, *not a fight.* This man had tried to reason with him and he had just refused to listen. He had gone on the offensive, charging the man, absolutely refusing to go with him when asked. He had dropped to the floor, his eyes closing, even as he did so.

"You didn't want to hit me, did you?" Tag asked the question but his voice held the certainty that he was correct.

"No, I didn't." His companion sat, his eyes on the floor. "Eat, Tag. Then, we'll talk. I am not an enemy. I want to help you. And you can help us."

Tag sat back at last, his eyes on the other man, just waiting.

"Okay, you brought me here. I want to know why. And just who are you?"

"I am a friend, Tag. We have worked together before but you wouldn't have known that. You were one of the patrol officers assigned to help break up that huge smuggling group." The man watched as Tag nodded. "My name is Shay, or Shane on the street. This time? We need your help once again. We know who it is that kidnapped you and Ayron and forced you to marry. We know why. We just have to find him and arrest him."

"Shay? I remember hearing that name. You're young to be up that far in the firm."

"I know. I started working for them when I was a teenager. I can't discuss what I have been involved with. But this with Ayron? If we had known in time, we would have prevented it."

Tag shook his head. "You're not in control of that. God is. He's allowed it and I don't know why. But I want to find Ayron. Do you know where she is?"

"We do, but it is like a fortress. She is on an island in the middle of a lake not far from here. The only access is by boat. We need to plan, Tag, and plan well."

"I get that. Evan had something like that happen to Flannery. Friends went in and found her and Eunice's daughter and brought them out. Now, talk. I want to know who and why."

Shay nodded. "I can do that. First, can we pray? We need to do that. We need to bathe your lady in prayer, for protection. The man who has her is vicious and will stop at nothing to get what he wants."

"And that would be?" Tag didn't like how Shay hesitated for a moment.

"Revenge. Plain and simple. Revenge."

Chapter 38

Tag paced the bedroom he had taken to, not willing to sleep but knowing at some point that he had to. At Shay's suggestion, he had sent a text to Brownie and his father, letting them know that he was fine but that he had a lead on where Ayron was. He had to follow it. Tag let them know that he would be in touch, as soon as it was possible.

Shay had watched him walk away that evening, his heart heavy. He didn't know if they would be in time to rescue Ayron. A fellow officer was watching the island, monitoring who was coming and going. It was coming to a crisis point when they would be moving in to make the arrests but Ayron's life was at stake. He just didn't know if Tag would stay in the background and let them bring her home. Shay knew that if he had been in Tag's place, he would not stay back. He would want to be right in front, leading the charge.

Early the next morning, Tag reached for his phone. It had been chiming off and on all night and he had ignored it. He smiled grimly at the messages from Brownie, worry foremost in the texts but also relaying information on their search. His father hadn't said much, other than that they were still working on the case and that they were praying for him.

Shay turned from the door that he had been staring out of as Tag walked his way. Today? They would spend in planning. Shay had been given permission by his supervisor to lay it all out for Tag, but he really wasn't sure if Tag was physically up to it.

"Shay? Where do we stand? And when do we go in?" Tag wasted no time in approaching Shay.

"We plan today, Tag. Word is that he has gone back down south for a day or so."

"You must have someone on the inside to know that." Tag's hand went up. "I know how it works, Shay."

"I can't confirm or deny that, Tag. Let's eat and then we can start working. Others on my team are doing the same. And yes, we are watching the island. If we need to, we'll move in today."

"But you're not ready to, is what you're not saying." Tag walked to the kitchen, reaching for the coffee pot and looking at it. "How many pots of coffee will we need today?"

"Probably too many." Shay cleared the dishes away from their quick meal and then reached for his laptop and the pile of folders he had set on the counter. "Pray first, Tag, and then we work."

Tag nodded, his head bowing, knowing that it would be God who got them through this and brought out his lady love. He missed her. Her sense of humour and quick responses to his teasing brightened his day and he missed that, very much.

Sitting back mid-afternoon, Tag stared at the pile of notes and then made a decision. He pulled out his phone and found the picture of the parchment.

"We found this in the secret room, Shay. I can't read it or even begin to understand what it is. I did send on a photo to a friend whose wife handles parchments like these."

"Have you heard back from her?" Shay studied the photo. "This is a missing piece of our puzzle, Tag. I can make out enough to know that this goes back to Ayron's great-grandfather. It's a deed to land that she never knew was hers. And it's right outside of town."

"Is that what he's after? What is on that land?"

"There have been rumours of a buried treasure." Shay's grin lit up his face for a moment. "I know. It sounds like something out of a movie, but that's what we're hearing. It goes to Ayron through her mother's lineage. It is a nice piece of property and in itself worth millions."

"It is? Is that what he's after? But I don't understand. If he is, why force us to marry?"

"That we can finally answer. He was out for revenge, Tag, plain and simple revenge again her father. He wanted to marry her to his son but her father refused. I am not sure if he knew the man was evil or not. And as to you? It's what we thought. You were involved in the raid that time and he found out your name. He should not have done that. He wanted revenge against you as well. This is how his warped mind decided to do just that. Force you two to marry. If you had not, he really would have killed her."

"That's what I don't fully understand. If he killed her, what did he get?"

"His home has been searched. We found a will that he has forged, with her signature on it, leaving everything she owned to him. He didn't think that you would agree to the marriage. He is now trying to still get what she has. If you die, then she needs a new heir. That would be him."

"And her lawyer was involved?"

"He was. The couple that said that they bought her house? Related to him as well. They have planned this for years, likely since her mother passed away."

"That is just sick, you know. Just plain sick." Tag rose and paced, his heart breaking for his lady. Please, Lord, protect her. Bring her home to me. I love her more than anything here on earth. I want a chance to tell her that and see if she feels the same.

Tag turned and stared at Shay. "Now what? Where do we go? We can't wait that long to go in and get her."

"No, we can't. Plans are being made. You and I will wait here, Tag. My team goes in tonight and brings her out."

"And where do they bring her to? I will accept nothing other than that she is with me."

"We understand that, Tag, and will do that. Here for now, and then we find somewhere else."

Tag nodded and then walked away, needing to find a prayer corner and spend the next hours in prayer for his lady and for the team. He knew it would be dangerous. Just how dangerous was the question.

Chapter 39

Cowering in the corner of the room, Ayron covered her head with her arms, not wanting to hear the shouting in the other rooms. She jumped as she heard gunfire. *Please, Lord, protect me. Help me to escape. Only I'm on an island and I have no idea if there are boats or any way off of it.* She didn't look up as she heard the door slam open. A hand on her arm caused her to scream even as she struggled to release herself.

"It's okay, Ayron. We're friends." The calm voice finally reached through her terror. "We've come to take you away from here. And to Tag. Tag's with a friend of ours."

She was led from the cabin, out of a back door and then quickly to a motorboat. Shoved aboard and told to lay flat on the deck, she did so, her arms covering her head once more. She felt the boat rock as men jumped aboard and then the boat moving across the lake. Ayron didn't know when she had been more scared, unable to pray even. The man who had helped her escape reached for her arm and helped her to the dock.

"This way, Ayron. We need to get you out of sight and undercover and quickly."

Ayron felt the coat thrown over her head and ducked, not sure what was really happening, other than that she was free.

"Find Terry. Find my neighbour. He's the one." Her words were whispered as she was shoved this time into a car.

"We know, Ayron. We know. We've been working on finding the evidence that we need to arrest him. Kidnapping you? He signed away his freedom. We'll find him. And soon. My team is working on that."

"And just who is your team?" Ayron spun on the car seat, to stare at the older man. A frown covered her face for a moment. "I know you. You've been around town. I think Dad spoke with you at some point."

"I have been. And yes, your father did. He was worried about you. He had heard rumours that something was to happen to you, but couldn't find the source or even a confirmation of what was planned." He shook his head as she opened her mouth. "We'll answer your questions all in good time. We still have some investigations to do. And yes, Tag is aware of this as is his supervisor and the men and ladies of your town police force. It has been a long process, Ayron, and should soon be over."

"Was Terry the one who made Tag marry me? I don't get why." Ayron wrapped her arms around her abdomen, staring out into the night.

"He was, Ayron. We're sorry that we could not prevent that. He would have killed you. Are you aware that you have a large plot of land worth millions outside of your town?"

Ayron spun once more to stare at him, shock on her face, her eyes huge.

"I had no idea. That can't be right. Dad would have told me."

"He would have. It is to come to you when you are thirty, unless you marry before then. And then, by the will that your mother left, it would go to your husband if something happened to you."

"My mother? I don't understand." Ayron frowned at him. "And if my husband were to die? Then what?"

"Then we know he had a will forged that would leave it to him."

"Archer again. Just like my house. What was in it for him?"

"Money more than likely. Archer had plans to move away from here. He worked this from when you were young, before your mother died, by what we can determine."

Ayron stared at him and then looked away, sorrow briefly flickering across her face, before she set it in impassive lines.

"Tag? Is he okay?"

The man with her, Samuel by name, smiled. "He is. He fought the man sent to bring him to us and ended up knocked out again."

"Oh, now!" Ayron's cry of dismay was torn from her. "How many more head injuries will he have to suffer? He's hurting enough as it is. He won't be going back to the police force. We've talked."

"No, he won't be. But we'll find something for him to do." Samuel studied the area around him.

"We're almost there, Ayron. Soon you'll be with Tag. We'll keep you together."

"And what about Brownie and our friends? Tag's family? They'll wonder where we are." Ayron was not backing down, not yet anyway.

"We've alerted them to what is happening and that you are both safe."

"Safe? You call this safe?" Ayron's voice rose as she spoke, drawing all eyes in the vehicle to her. "I wouldn't call it very safe. Kidnapped. Dropped on an island. Threatened. Rescued by men who say they are the good guys. Told Tag is safe. How do I know that?"

Samuel had begun to grin as she spoke, knowing that she was venting and that she needed to.

"Right here, Ayron. This road here leads us to the cabin. Tag is there with Shay."

"He is? And how soon do we get there?" She watched as a beautiful log cabin came into view. "This is it?"

"It is. Here, out you go. Tag is inside, watching for you." Samuel watched as Ayron stood for a moment, her eyes on the cabin, before she ran for it, Shay holding open the door, and pointing towards the kitchen.

Tag began to turn as he heard running footsteps, a lady's by the sounds of it, he thought. He barely had time to brace himself before a body hit him, making him stagger, and then arms were wrapped tight around his neck, almost too tight. His arms wrapped around the lady, knowing that it was Ayron. Tag felt her tears soaking into his shirt and his own eyes filled to the point that he could barely see Shay in front of him. He sent a low thank you to Shay before he gathered Ayron close and then found the chair he had begun to think of his. It was enough, for the moment, that Ayron was there and in his arms. His praise to God began as well as a plea for it all to be resolved so that they could go on with their lives.

Chapter 40

His eyes on Ayron's face, Tag watched as she drifted off to sleep, feeling safe and secure in his arms. His heart was raised in prayer for protection for his lady, and he thought through every verse that he could remember about protection and being safe. He begged God for that, to protect her. At long last, Tag rose, cradling Ayron to him and headed for the bedroom that he had been told to use.

Tucking her under a blanket, Tag dropped to his knees, his arms around her, his head on hers as he continued his petition. He rose at long last, his eyes focused on the wall in front of him, before he headed for the door. Closing it quietly behind him, Tag pulled out his phone and then headed for Shay and Samuel, who looked up at his coming and nodded to one another.

"Samuel, is it? Thank you. I won't ask how or where. I know that's part of the investigation." Tag paused for a moment, his emotions getting the best of him. "Where do we stand? And I have had a lot of information coming at me." He held up his phone.

"Emails?" At Tag's nod, Shay reached for the laptop. "Here. You can sign in on this one. Share what you can. And then we need to talk."

Tag sorted through the emails, rising to gather what he had printed, still not sure of Shay or Samuel. He stopped, praying harder than he had in his life, he thought. *Lord, we need to end this and soon. Ayron needs Your protection. I fear for her very life. This man, her neighbour, is brutal. But there is someone else.*

"Shay, this is what I have. I still think that there is someone else. Someone running the show."

"There is, Tag." Samuel spoke, his eyes on the material that Tag handed him. "This proves it. Did you see this?" He held up one piece of paper.

Tag nodded. "I did. I don't like that. How compromised is the investigation?"

"We don't know, not yet. I sent Bruce in to speak with Brownie and his chief. I have also contacted Eric. We had these suspicions before, just needed proof. We know have that."

"We do." Tag sank into his chair, absentmindedly reaching for his mug of cold coffee. "Where do we go from here?"

"First, we do everything in our power to keep both you and Ayron safe. That means keeping you two tucked away. Here for now but we will move you if we need to." Samuel studied Tag and then nodded. "Ayron must go along with us. It means her life and your life if she doesn't."

"I need to speak with my father, just to find out where he stands on the investigation." Tag stared at Samuel, almost not blinking.

"We can do that, Tag. Not your phone but one of ours." Samuel looked down, studying the mass of papers in front of him. "This is the point where a novelist would call it the crisis. We have to get you both through this and God willing, we will."

"I know, Samuel, that you will try your best. But God is in control." Tag shifted the papers, finding the one he wanted. "This bit about Terry? How far back does it go?"

"His involvement in white-collar crime? Back to his early twenties. Likely thirty years or more. He has hidden it well."

"He has. I don't understand how Ayron's father missed that."

"He's good at pretending, Tag." Samuel's gaze shifted to watch Ayron as she stopped. "We have been able to reach out to those in the surrounding towns that he cheated and stole from. He didn't do it in Lakeside, in order to keep his reputation clean here and not be suspected. He also used a number of aliases."

Tag jumped slightly as he felt an arm along his shoulders and then just simply reached to wrap an arm around Ayron, pulling her close to him.

"Who in town then do we talk with?"

"You don't. Not now. Brownie said his chief had arranged for Dooley and Eunice to do that. It's not unusual."

"No, it's not." Tag's eyes were on Ayron. "Ayron, my love? What is it?"

"Terry? He played us, as they say. I know that Dad had begun to withdraw from him, not going back and forth for meals and coffee as he used to. Is this why? He had picked up on something?"

"I suspect that he has. Would your father have documented anything?" Shay watched her closely even as he asked the question.

Ayron stared at Shay for a moment, thinking through his question. She shook her head.

"I doubt it. I went through all his paperwork, pulled what was in the safety deposit box, and found nothing that way. I didn't find anything about that property you tell me I own. I should have. Can we see if Archer went into the bank and pulled it? And if he went through the house, he could have found that paperwork as well and taken it."

Shay and Samuel shared a look before they both looked at Tag, to find him watching them closely. Tag nodded, knowing that steps had already been taken.

"We have served warrants on his home and office, Ayron." Shay spoke hesitantly. "We had thought of something like this, given what he has already tried with you."

"I see. How long will that take, to go through his places?" Ayron moved away from Tag, heading for the coffee pot. She made a fresh pot, standing to watch the water drip into the pot before she filled her own mug and then refilled the men's.

Samuel had been watching her, seeing just how close to the edge she was. We need this over, Lord, and today. Only I don't think it will be.

"They've been through and gathered everything. They have it at our headquarters going through it."

Ayron nodded and then headed for the back door, through it before any of the men reply. Tag sat and watched the closed door, wanting to go to her but knowing that she just needed time to absorb what she had been told.

Chapter 41

Two days later, Tag watched Ayron pace the area at the back of the cabin before he approached her, wrapping her into a hug. She hesitated and then hugged him back, her head resting against him.

"Tag? Can we go home? It's not going to end with us tucked away."

"I know, my love. I know. We need to do something to bring the culprits out. Shay told me a bit ago that they were getting close and had the warrants ready that they needed to serve."

"But Terry will stay away when he finds out I am missing. He has other properties, I think, not likely under his own name." Ayron stared around. "This is close to town, you know."

"It is? I didn't know that." Tag stared at her and then at the path that led to the lake. "How game are you to walk?"

"As game as you are. Let's move." Ayron walked away, leaving Tag staring at her before he ran to catch up.

"We should leave a note or something."

"Send Shay a text message. We're heading home, or at least, I hope we are." Ayron would not tell Tag just how afraid that she was.

Tag pocketed his phone, knowing that Shay would be angry with them. But this was their life, and they needed to move on. That couldn't happen, or at least, he didn't think it could, while they were hiding.

Shay stared at his phone before he handed it to Samuel. After reading Tag's message, Samuel nodded. They had done what both Shay and he had expected, headed home. It was not what they had wanted but he knew that they were taking steps to protect themselves and also solve it to move on with their lives.

Tag watched the house for a moment, seeing movement, and then feeling relief. His father was here and likely had been for the last couple of days.

Thurlow turned as he heard Tag's voice.

"Tag? You two are okay?"

"We are now, Dad. Let's move inside." Tag waited for Ayron to move towards the house, puzzled as to why she didn't. "Ayron?"

"Something's wrong with the house, Tag. I just can't go in." Ayron jumped as his arms surrounded her.

"That's the feeling I had, Ayron." Thurlow spoke up. "I had just called for Brownie and his team to come. They'll go through it for us. I know that you have a security system and that Brownie would have set it after Tag disappeared, but someone could still have tampered with it. Into my truck. We'll wait there for him. And you two can tell me what was going on."

They watched as Brownie and his team searched the outside of the house before moving inside. Tag sighed. This was not how he planned on bringing Ayron home. Not at all.

"Dad, what can you tell us?"

"About whom? Archer? Terry? The couple? They are all in this together. Your property, Ayron? The one coming to you from your mother. Your mother had sold it just before she died. We found documentation that stated she felt it best. The money from it? Your father put it into a trust fund for you. If you refuse it, then it goes to charities."

"She did? I'm glad. I don't want it. But I don't know of any property being developed around here."

"No, it hasn't yet. The buyer agreed to wait until you reached thirty or married. He can now move ahead with his plans. His plans? To develop it for housing for low-income families. He plans to make a village there." Thurlow glanced back at her. "He has asked to meet with you. He would like your input on the planning."

"He would? Then I guess so. I wonder if this is what Dad wanted to speak with me about but we never got a chance to."

"It could be, Ayron. Brownie did say that they found a letter to you from your parents, that Archer had somehow managed to take from the house."

"He did? Will I never be free of him?"

"Soon, we pray, Ayron. Soon." Thurlow rolled down his window as Brownie approached. "Brownie? Somehow, I don't like the look on your face."

Brownie shook his head, his eyes on Ayron. "No, you won't. It's a good thing that you didn't go in. There was a bomb set to go off at the back door and one at the office door and one outside near the garage. Overkill, I know, but that's exactly what they wanted to do. Kill you, Ayron and Tag. These were sent as a message. We are thankful that no one was hurt."

Ayron stared at him, shocked for a moment. She felt Tag's hand tighten on hers.

"Who?"

"That we will work on. Your security camera has picked up movement. We'll take a look at it."

"Terry. Arthurs, if he is in the area. But there is someone else, isn't there?" Ayron stared at her home. "When does this end? When I am dead and buried? When Tag is? When someone innocent is killed?"

Chapter 42

Standing in the kitchen doorway later that morning, Thurlow watched Tag and Ayron as they faced one another. He could see the anger in both of them, not at one another, but at the circumstances and danger that they faced. Sparks were flying between the two and he had seen the looks of love and longing for things to be different that they were throwing towards each other. Lord, he prayed, please let this be over. These two need to get on with their lives and don't feel that they can, not until this is resolved. Thurlow had talked with them, directed them to the verses that spoke of protection, of safety. He had also shown them the verses that directed them each to seek the Lord in all ways, to be able to understand in part the path they had had to walk.

Tag finally spoke, his hands reaching for Ayron's, his grasp strong and tight, conveying to her his love. She frowned for a moment before her face softened and her love for him stood in her eyes.

"Dad? How do we draw out the man or woman behind this? Do we even know who?"

Thurlow walked towards them, setting down his laptop and folders that he had retrieved from his truck.

"We do. Emma and Jace have come through. They have given me a name, which I have not passed on as yet. And your friend, Finn? She has emailed me about that parchment."

"That parchment? The one I didn't see?" Ayron turned to him. "What is going on with that?"

"That, my dear, is not what we seemed to think it was. It was an old document that really had nothing to do with you or your property. At first glance, that's what it seemed, but Finn has researched it. It is for property far away from here and that has nothing to do with you or your family."

"Then why here?"

"I suspect that Terry left it there or Arthurs. For what reason, we may never know. Terry has been arrested in our town, Tag, and faces numerous charges there and in other municipalities."

"He really is?" Ayron sighed. "And Dad thought he was a friend. We spent a lot of time going back and forth." She stopped speaking, her eyes on Tag. "His wife? The one that only was around once in a while? What about her?"

"He was never married, Ayron. Just pretended to be. That woman? We think that she is the one behind all of this."

"A woman?" Tag sank into his chair at the table, eyes on his father. "That makes sense, you know. A woman could be this evil."

"They can be." Ayron leaned against the counter, her eyes on the floor. "How do we find her?"

"We have, Ayron. Abe and his team have found her. He was sending the information to Brownie and also Eric. Dooley's chief was to get it as well. She is in the area."

"That means we have to stay hidden?" Ayron blew out a deep breath. "For how long?"

"Not long, I pray." Thurlow pointed to the chairs. "Sit for a moment, Ayron. I know that you feel as if all we are doing to talking. But there is something there we have missed. And I need to go back over some things with you."

Ayron stared at him and then spun, heading for the hallway. The men could hear her footsteps on the stairs and then walking from room to room. Tag sat with a puzzled look on his face, not quite sure what was going on, but trusting Ayron enough to know that she would speak with them when she was clear in her mind with her thoughts.

"Tag? How much were you told?" Thurlow's quiet question brought Tag's attention to himself.

"A lot, Dad. Most of it, I think. I know of Shay from other areas. He's worked undercover before with this force. Samuel? I don't know him but I wasn't picking up anything wrong there. What do you need to know?"

"Tell me what they said, what they felt, where they were headed. I know it's an investigation that I am not part of, but please, son. Let me know what you can."

Tag nodded, his eyes on the kitchen doorway where Ayron stood once more. His hand held out to her moved her feet forward as her hand reached for his and she sat.

"I would like to know too, Tag. What can you tell that won't damage anything?"

Tag sighed. "There are some things that I can tell you. Dad has said most of it. In fact, Dad, I think you are ahead of Shay and his friends."

"I am? How?"

"Emma. Jace. Finn. Abe sent me a text and said that one of his friends was heading this way with more material for you. His team is off somewhere training another team and he felt it best not to wait."

"Okay. Tully is still working away. I heard from Dooley earlier today. He has been working it on his own as has Eunice. Evan is weighing in as well. It's a race between us and Shay's team to see who finishes it off first."

"I pray it is us." Ayron's face grew sad. "I miss Mom and Dad at this point. I just need my Mom."

Tag gave a low sound and wrapped her in his arms. His eyes raised to his father.

"Dad? Can we get Mom to come up?"

Thurlow gave a small smile, sadness in his heart for his young daughter-in-law. "She's on her way. When I spoke to her earlier about what we found and that you were here, she just stated that she was on her way. Tully's are coming with her."

"Good. We can brainstorm." Tag's eyes were on Ayron. "And just maybe between us all, we can solve this." Hi watched as Ayron's head raised, a faraway look in her eyes. "Ayron, my love, what did you remember?"

Ayron shook for a moment in her fear. "I know who it is. And she's brutal. Always has been. She's our age, Tag. How can that be?"

Chapter 43

Tully handed Tag a report that he had just found in the paperwork that he had been handed by Jace. His face was grim as he did so. Tag stared at him and then down at the paperwork.

"It's that bad, Tully?"

"It is." Tully searched for Ayron. "And it involves someone who called themselves her friend. This is going to hurt."

Tag nodded as he read through the report. "Actually, we've talked about her. Ayron tried to avoid her, didn't want anything to do with her, but she kept showing up, telling people that they were best friends." Tag sighed. "And she's in town, right?"

"She is. We've looked at her family. Her father was the one who started this and she took it over. It has just grown since then. They have ties to Terry, cousins of a kind I think, distant ones."

"Who are you talking about, Tully?" Ayron read over Tag's shoulder. "Her? No, I couldn't stand her. I always felt evil around her. She tried to play that we were friends but everyone in town knew different. Now, how do we catch her?"

"No, you're not going out there to meet her. Not yet." Thurlow reached for the paperwork and scanned it. "This goes with what Brownie and Eunice have found."

"I can't do this much longer. I just can't." Tag's arms around her kept her beside him.

"We know, my love. We know that. Just work with us? Dad has some ideas. So do Brownie, Evan and Eunice. Let's hear them out and see what we can come up with."

An hour later, Tag stared down at his notes, confident that they had come up with a plan, but not that confident that Ayron or even he himself would be safe. There was just so much uncertainty about it all.

"Tag? Tomorrow?" Thurlow watched his son closely.

"I think so, Dad. If we can draw her out and I am sure that we will be able to, then hopefully it will be all over tomorrow." He searched the messages on his phone. "Abe said his team is available tomorrow and will head here tonight. They won't contact us, but they will know where we are and where we are heading."

"He can do that?" Ayron shook her head and then rose, her eyes on the clock. "We need to eat, people. Brownie? You up to doing the grilling?"

Brownie grinned at her, a task that he had done many times with her father and herself.

"That I am. The meat is in the freezer or the fridge?"

"The fridge. Meg made a grocery run earlier as we tossed everything that was in the fridge and freezer."

The men froze in their movements before their eyes went to the four ladies, seeing Eunice nodding.

"It had to be done, guys." Eunice moved to help Brownie. "We have no way of knowing what would have been tampered with."

Late that evening, Ayron sought her comfort spot, the swing on the back deck. Her head back, she watched the clouds scudding across the sky, briefly hiding the moon and the stars. She could hear the birds and insects before her mind drifted back in time, to when her mother was alive. She missed her so much. Ayron decided that she just needed her mother, given the danger that she was in and also to walk her along the path of her first love. And love Tag she did. How she would ever walk away from him when this was over, she wasn't sure of, but knew that she had to. Ayron had seen glimpses of his feelings for her and he would persist in calling her his love but she just didn't know exactly how he felt.

Tag watched from the kitchen door, the lights on low behind him. The house was quiet, everyone leaving to seek their rest, to be ready to come back in the morning and spent time in prayer and seeking God's protection. He knew that they could not do it on their own. Even with God in the picture, he thought, it was still dangerous. Tag feared losing Ayron to the mad woman as she persisted in calling her.

Sinking down beside her on the swing, his arm drawing her to him, Tag pushed his toes at the floor to set the swing in motion. He didn't say anything, not at first, and then began to speak, telling Ayron of his dreams and wishes from when he was a child. He couldn't look at her as he continued, telling her about the lady that he had dreamed of all those years, the lady who God would provide to share his life and be his helpmeet. He felt her tense before he sighed.

"You're the lady, Ayron. You are the very lady that I dreamt about. God brought us together, even given the circumstances. I just wanted you to know before tomorrow that I love you deeply and always will." Tag dropped a kiss on her temple and then rose, heading back into the house, to seek his rest. He would not sleep until Ayron had sought her own, that was a given.

Ayron stood, watching Tag walk away, knowing that he had just laid his heart out for her to see. And it was up to her to decide what she wanted to do. She knew in her heart what that was. Ayron just wasn't sure if that was God's plan for her.

Chapter 44

Tag was up and about early the next morning. To say that his sleep had been broken and poor would have been an understatement. He had spent a good portion of his awake time in prayer, petitioning and seeking God's help in their plans. He felt confident that they were moving in the way they should, but as an officer, Tag knew there were many things that could and would go wrong or different from what they had planned. He had watched the car parked across the street from the house, knowing that they were being watched.

Ayron paused as she saw Tag standing at the kitchen counter, his head bowed, before she moved towards him, his hand coming out for hers.

"Are we ready, Tag?"

"I think so. As much as we can be, I suspect. You know that it won't go exactly as we planned." He grinned as she snorted.

"Nothing ever goes exactly as planned, now does it? We have prepared. We have people around us. God is going before us and is around us, sheltering us with His hand. Nothing will happen to us that He doesn't allow."

"I know, my love. I just worry that you will be killed. I don't know that I could go on if you are."

Ayron blinked rapidly, tears momentarily blinding her. "Thank you, Tag. We do need to talk. But what you said last night? You're the knight in shining armour that Mom always wove into my bedtime stories. You're the one that Dad described to me not many months before he went home, telling me to wait for the one God had chosen for me." Tag's eyes had turned to her as she spoke. "So you see, I do love you too. We need to make it through today and then talk." She moved away from him as the front door opened.

Thurlow watched closely as Tag and Ayron walked down the street in her hometown, pausing to glance in windows and then moving on again. He could see them being greeted and knew that Ayron would be introducing Tag to them. His eyes lifted and he saw her, watching his son and his wife walk towards her.

"Is that her, Dad?" Tully had his camera up, recording their walk.

"It is. We'll need to get closer."

"No, Dad. That's not the plan. We need to let Brownie do that, him and his fellow officers. I have seen some of Abe's men following them. They'll keep them under observation and keep as close as they can."

"I know, Tully." Thurlow blew out a deep breath, his fingers tapping on the steering wheel. "It just doesn't make it any easier."

Ayron looked up at last, her steps slowing. Tag looked at her and then at the woman standing in front of them. *This is it, isn't it, Lord? The moment of reckoning? Protect my lady, that's all I ask.*

"Jean Wilson! I am not surprised to see you. You've dogged my steps for so many years." Ayron went on the offensive, not quite what they had planned.

"Ayron! Who on earth calls anyone such a ridiculous name! Yes, I am here. And yes, you will pay."

"Pay? For what?" Ayron shook her head. "I'm sorry. I don't think I have anything to pay."

"But you do." A gun appeared in Jean's hands. "Now, you two are going to head into that building right beside you. We have some talking to do."

Ayron felt Tag's hand tighten on hers. "I don't think so, Jean. We have nothing to talk about. We never did. Do you think I want anything to do with you?"

"Sure, you do. You have something that belongs to me and I want it." Jean moved closer, the gun wavering in her shaky hand.

"I don't think so. You can't get my land. It was sold before Mom died. The trust fund? It will go to good use. No one but myself can access it. If anyone else tries, it automatically goes into a charity."

"That's not true." Jean dug out a paper for her pocket. "This is what it says. That you can give it away."

"Who told you that? It's not true, never has been." Ayron stood her ground. "If it was your father, he should have known better. He's dead. Makes me wonder if you killed him because he told you the truth."

"No, it wasn't me. It was Archer. He killed Dad. Said that Dad was moving in on his territory or something like that."

"And just what did your father do?" Tag asked the question, seeing Abe's men and Brownie moving in.

"He was an accountant. A good one. Only her father would never use him."

"No, he wouldn't. He didn't trust him." Ayron moved back a few steps, taking Tag with her. "He was dishonest. That's why he worked with Arthurs. Just how much did your father steal?"

Tag drew in a breath at that question, seeing the venom now evident on Jean's face. Before he could move, the gun had discharged, hitting him in the shoulder and sending him to the ground, Ayron tumbling down with him. He heard faint shouts and calls and Ayron begging him to be all right before everything faded to darkness.

Ayron was on her knees, her hands on Tag's shoulder to try and stem the flow of blood. Matt, the paramedic on Abe's team, was beside her, assessing Tag and then reaching to help the town paramedics as they worked on him. Thurlow drew Ayron to her feet and stood, an arm around her, watching his son, his own face white. Tully's hand was on his father's shoulder before he turned, handing off his camera to Brownie, simply stating that he had filmed everything and that he thought he had the sound as well. Brownie nodded, a stern look on his face as he watched Jean walk away, her hands cuffed behind her.

"Is this is, Brownie?" Thurlow's voice was taut.

"I think so. We had everyone but her, and Jean is not who I suspected. Not at all."

"Tag talked to Shay and Samuel last night. She has been on their radar for the last few years. They regret that they were not able to move in before Tag and Ayron were forced to marry."

Brownie nodded, his eyes on Abe as he approached them. "Somehow, I don't think that would have worked. God's timing is God's timing. He knew this would happen and prepared us for it. Now, off you three go. We'll catch up with you in a while.

Chapter 45

Tag moved restlessly that night on the hospital bed. He had some pain, but not what he had expected to have when he was informed that he had been shot. It was a lucky shot, the surgeon said, just staring at Tag when Tag shook his head and said, no, that God had directed the course of the bullet.

Ayron watched him before she moved to stand beside him, her hand on his face, her other hand in his. She was thankful that Tag had not been hurt worse but angry that it had come to that. Then, she sighed. *I know, Lord, I know. Anger doesn't work. I need to seek Your peace and comfort and understand just why You allowed this to happen.*

Tag watched her face, seeing the peace that gradually came over it. *Lord, I need that peace as well and I am not sure that I can find it. Not as quickly as Ayron has done.*

"Tag? You're okay?" Ayron's voice was low. It was after visiting hours and she didn't want to be asked to leave.

"I am. I could have gone home, but we decided that I should stay, remember? Just until Brownie and his team get things sorted out overnight."

"Do we have them all?" Ayron blew out a breath. "What about her children? Her husband walked away from her before the second one was born and has refused any contact with them or her."

"Brownie was working on that. He'll look after them." Tag yawned. "I'm sorry. The pain medications are kicking in. I am so tired of them."

"I know, sweetheart. I know. I don't like having to see you take them, not when I'm the cause of it." She watched as he slept before she kissed his cheek and then turned to find the chair that the nurses had brought in for her.

The next afternoon, Tag stood and stared at his father, not quite sure that he had heard him correctly.

"Who did you say, Dad? Who did you say was her husband?"

"Jack Barton from your force. Do you remember her at all?"

Tag shook his head. "Not at all. But I didn't know Jack all that much. Just saw him around the detachment. We always worked different shifts, and he went undercover in the drug squad." Tag's eyes slid closed. "Is that part of it?"

"We think so. Her father seems to have had fingers in many pies, and the drug trade in our town was one of them. I don't know that Jack knew this. Brownie spoke with him last night and he is on his way to pick up his children. They will need prayer, Tag. They don't know their father at all."

"And Jean? What about her?"

"Jean? She won't stand trial." Thurlow's hand went up as he saw the look on Ayron's face. "She decided to overdose last night. We don't know where she got the drugs but she did somehow. The Lord has dealt with her."

———

216

"He has. I feel sorry for her children. I can't image how they were raised." Ayron walked away, leaving Tag staring after her, his hand resting on the sling.

"She'll be okay, Tag. Just needs some time."

"And I know who she can talk to, if it comes to that." Tag turned back to his father. "You're heading home today?"

"We are. Tully and Lia have already headed out. Mom was waiting to talk with Ayron and then we're on our way." Thurlow reached to hug his son, knowing that the bullet could very well have killed him.

Tag went searching for Ayron, seating himself beside her in the swing, an arm drawing her close to him.

"This is it, Tag? We don't have to watch for anyone else?"

"Not that I know of. We'll take a few days, my love, and then Brownie said he'd be around, just to update us on the charges." Tag drew a deep breath, feeling the strain and stress and tension leaving his body. "We'll get there, my love."

"I know, Tag. I know. It's just been a horrible few weeks in some ways."

"That it has. Now, I just want to sit and cuddle with my bride and enjoy the afternoon, without worrying about anything."

Chapter 46

Brownie watched Tag and Ayron as they walked towards him as he waited outside the police detachment. He shook his head. They were not watching what was going on around them, that much he could tell. He looked at the sky and then nodded. Yes, they had everyone, thankfully. That part of their adventure was over. Now to finish off what he could tell them.

Tag looked up, a grin on his face as he saw his friend waiting. Eric had called, telling him that Brownie would let them know what he could for everyone. And he wanted Tag to come back. Only Tag didn't know that he would. He liked life in this small town. He felt he could find something to do that he would enjoy. Tag knew that Ayron would move if he really insisted but he had no desire to ask that of her.

"Brownie? You're waiting for us. Good news or bad news?"

Ayron shook her head at Tag. "It has to be good news. He's got his happy face on."

Tag stared down at her and then at Brownie, who shrugged, an answering grin on his face.

"Happy news, Ayron. At long last, happy news for you. Let's walk. I think a meeting in the park would be just what we need."

———

218

Tag stared at the group gathered there. His family. Abe and his team and their wives. He saw Jacob and Finn and waved. He was happy, he thought, and content. He had a lady to love who loved him back, God was in his life, and he had friends and family around him.

A picnic meal was enjoyed before Ayron turned to Brownie.

"Brownie, what can you tell us? I know there are things that you can't."

"You are correct, Ayron. There are things that will stay quiet as the investigations move forward and will come out in court. But I can tell you some of what we discovered." Brownie looked around, finding Thurlow watching him. "Thurlow, would you pray?"

Thurlow nodded, his prayer seeking assurance for them all that Tag and Ayron were safe, and that they would all continue to grow in their faith and trust in God.

"Okay, Ayron. Tag. Your marriage. It was Jean Wilson who set that up. She was so jealous of you, Ayron. You were popular, had parents who loved you. She knew about the money, her father had talked, and she felt that it should go to her. She arranged for you to be kidnapped and then for Tag to be the one you married. You are not aware, either one of you, that Tag was followed that day and that they let you escape Ayron, hoping that you would run to him. That's what you did. Tag was not to have been beaten, but the kidnappers decided on that when Tag refused to marry you or you, him.

"Now, as to the property. It was willed to your mother from her maternal grandmother. At the time that the will was written, property was cheap. No one of them ever expected it to grow in value. The contractor who purchased it knew of the history. He was a friend of your father but had moved to a different town to work. He's planning on returning here to work on that land. He did say that he would welcome any and all assistance you and Tag would give him. If it had not been sold, it would have gone to you and you could have decided what to do with it."

Tag looked around, knowing that there were answers that they might never find. He was content, he thought, once more. Brownie had stopped by the day prior, and given him a head's up that a job offer was heading his way. Tag had stared at him and shaken his head. No, he said, he had no idea what he wanted to do, not yet. He had to heal and that would take time, he knew.

Ayron moved among the people gathered, hugs and thanks for each one. Abe watched her for a moment and then nodded, his voice low as he spoke to Emma, asking her if she needed someone to work off site for her. Tag or Ayron would be good to train. Emma had stared up at him and then nodded herself, simply saying that she would consider that.

Epilogue

Three months later, Ayron turned as she felt Tag's hand on her shoulder and into his hug. She was so grateful for the man who was married to her, her groom as she called him, a man of upright character, honest and true, and a true leader in their faith. That faith had been shaken when they had gone through their adventure as they termed it, but it had strengthened over time. Both knew that God had chosen each for the other.

"You're home early, Tag? Was there a problem at the doctor's?" Ayron was concerned. Tag had been in for his checkup at their doctor and wasn't due home yet.

"Nope. Not a one. He told me that as far as he is concerned, I am healed. I do need to keep speaking with our minister, but that's not a problem. He challenges me and I need that. How was your afternoon?"

Ayron shrugged, suddenly shy about the work she had undertaken with the contractor.

"Phil was around. He likes the plans that I have been making. He wants me to work closely with the architect. We've been trying to keep it simple and easy to take care of. Working families need time with their children and each other, not on upkeep."

"I like how you think." Tag turned her towards their favourite spot, her swing, and drew her down beside him, cuddling her close. "I have made a decision, my love."

"And that would be?"

"James asked if I had ever thought of counselling. He thinks I would do well at that. He has given me something to think about."

"And he hasn't seen the college catalogues that you have gathered, has he? I agree with him. You can take online courses, work with Evan at either the camp or the home for now."

"That I can." Tag grew silent. "I never expected that day when I started my shift that I would be drawn into an adventure such as we were or that I would find the love of my life." Tag kissed her upraised face. "I love you, Ayron, more each day."

"And I you, Tag. You were truly my knight in shining armour that day. Any regrets about resigning?"

"None. Eric understood. Dad has asked if I want to work remotely for him. And Emma has approached me to work for her."

"Wow! All those offers? We need to pray."

"And we will. God has a plan and purpose for us, as Murphy would tell us, that we don't know about. I am content to wait for his leading."

They grew silent, content to be with one another, and content that God really did have a plan and purpose for them, one that they were seeking with all their hearts to find. They were thankful for praying friends and family, who didn't need to know the details in order to pray for them.

———

Dear Readers

Thank you for choosing to read The Seeker, the story of Taggart and his lady love, Ayron. Once again, they have driven the story, telling their story as they wished it to be told, not how I would have chosen. They, like all my characters, love to bring in beloved characters from other stories just to help solve their mystery.

How do you seek God? It is as individual as each one of us. All we can do is seek Him with all our hearts and He has promised that He will be found. That is something that we are sometimes remiss in doing. My characters are very good at reminding me of how to live and serve God.

Those characters that walked in? First, Abe and his team are found in the series, *His Guardians,* and yes, each one of the eight had their adventure. Darcy is found in the adventure that she shared with Doug in *The Heart of a Lion.* Evan and Flannery's story is *The Dreamer*, the first book in *His Dreamseekers* series. I love when they walk back and forth. It makes it interesting, to say the least. And Storm and Shay have both appeared in other stories, Storm in *Dallas: Called to Return* and Shay in *His Trust*, Book Six in *His Guardians.* Jacob and Finn's story can be found in the first of the Mistletoe Treasures book, *Mischief and Mayhem in Mistletoe.*

God bless each one of you. Continue to seek Him, knowing that He will be found.

Ronna

Lightning Source UK Ltd.
Milton Keynes UK
UKHW021602200721
387466UK00010B/433